MONEY. FAME. WHISKEY. SEX.

For Dash Conner, lead singer of The Devil's Share, everything he wanted was his for the asking. Whiskey. Drugs. Money. Sex. But not Lexi Grant. For the first time since he picked up a guitar, a girl was actually demanding he woo her. For a chance with her, Dash would do that and more.

Lexi Grant was no groupie. Just because the biggest rock star in the world smiled at her didn't mean she *had* to fall into bed with him— but it was going to be awfully hard to resist that impish smile and those tatted abs. Surely one night of fun wouldn't hurt anyone.

Unless that night ends with a broken condom.

For Lexi and Dash, that's just the beginning. Add an overly affectionate pit bull, a missing guitarist, a house full of sorority girls, a junkie ex-bandmate and an extreme aversion to Jäger, and it's either a recipe for disaster or true love.

PLAY NICE

L.P. Maxa

Book One of The Devil's Share

www.BOROUGHSPUBLISHINGGROUP.com

PUBLISHER'S NOTE: This is a work of fiction. Names, characters, places and incidents either are the product of the author's imagination or are used fictitiously. Any resemblance to actual events, locales, business establishments or persons, living or dead, is coincidental. Boroughs Publishing Group does not have any control over and does not assume responsibility for author or third-party websites, blogs or critiques or their content.

PLAY NICE
Copyright © 2015 L.P. Maxa

ISBN 978-1-942886-55-6

For my Daddy. Thank you for loving me and rock and roll.

ACKNOWLEDGMENTS

First and foremost I need to thank my wonderful little family. My daughter for making me smile when I'm having a bad day. My husband for being so supportive and understanding when pics of half-naked rock stars that I'd screenshot would scroll across our computer screensaver. My mom who has been so incredibly into this since the first book I wrote. I couldn't have done this without her. All my amazing friends! You guys so selflessly share all the embarrassing, yet hilarious, details of your lives. You give me things to write about. Ang, thanks for having such a rock star of a little brother. You two were the inspiration behind *Play Nice*. My work people who fill my days with laughter and love to read romance novels as much as I do. You keep me writing even when I'm supposed to be doing something else. My favorite teacher of all time, Mrs. French, you're the best. My editor, who likes my book and thinks I'm funny. Thank you for making this an amazing process. I am truly the luckiest girl in the world to have such a supportive and encouraging group of people surrounding me on a daily basis.

CONTENTS

PLAY NICE

"Don't you know people write songs about girls like you?"

— The Naked and Famous

Chapter One

Lexi

"Isn't this so great?!"

I leaned closer to my best friend Amy. "What? I can't hear you?!"

"It's not *that* loud. I swear, Lex, you are aging prematurely."

I just shrugged and wrinkled my nose. If either of us was aging prematurely it was Amy. We were both only twenty-seven and I was almost positive that this was the first time she'd been out past ten in a couple of years. "It's just so loud. And people keep popping my personal-space bubble." I had been to my fair share of concerts before, but I had never been backstage at a venue like this one. This was a whole new experience. There were people everywhere—guys pushing around crates and carrying equipment, men in business suits talking on cell phones, people with press badges and cameras, girls wearing next to nothing and looking pretty happy about it. It was like a circus.

Amy shook her head. "Well I couldn't be happier. I mean, my baby brother is a rock star! All his dreams are literally coming true as we speak."

Amy and I had been best friends since our freshman year of college, almost ten years now. Her little brother Luke just joined one of the hottest bands in the nation, The Devil's Share. These guys were rockers through and through. They'd been nominated for several Grammys over the years. But if you listened to the press tell it, the band usually snubbed their noms. They played for the fans, for the love of the music. They rarely did any press or interviews. That was part of their allure, I was sure. Mysterious rock stars? Who could resist?

Lukey (that's what we called him) was a drummer, an amazing drummer. The band fired their original drummer Jared—according to rumor he couldn't kick the heroin—and held open auditions for his replacement in almost every major city in the nation picking Luke out of thousands of hopefuls. Amy was a rock groupie even before Luke had gotten the gig of a lifetime touring with The Devil's Share. Amy and Luke's dad had been a pretty well-known musician back in the day; they grew up around music, concerts and the rock lifestyle. I knew *of* The Devil's Share. I heard their songs on the radio. I liked them. Who wouldn't? Their music was solid, and they were all fucking gorgeous. And sexy. Plus, they were playing in Austin, where I lived. Going to a concert gave Amy an excuse to come visit and us a chance to see Luke play close to home.

"Oh. My. God!!! Look at my baby brother. I have never felt more proud of anything or anyone in my entire life!"

Amy dragged me over to the side of the stage where we could watch Luke play. I looked past the guys towards the sea of screaming fans. I couldn't help but tear up a little. Luke was one of the sweetest most compassionate guys I'd ever known and one of my dearest friends. If anyone deserved this, it was him. I let my eyes drift back to the stage. "Amy, he looks perfect out there." I'd seen Luke play a million times, but this was different. Luke's shaggy blonde hair moved with every beat of his drums. He was smiling like a five-year-old on Christmas morning. This was his tenth stop on his first tour with the band, and you could tell he was loving every minute of it.

The first song ended and the lead singer, Dash, looked over in our direction. He had dark, messy hair that had that perpetual I-just-ran-my-fingers-through-it look. His tight black pants left little to the imagination, his loose black t-shirt showed off his muscular arms, which were covered in tattoos. I drank in the sight of his body, wanting to sit down and spend an hour memorizing the artwork. Our eyes met and my stomach dropped to my feet. His gaze set my insides on fire. I couldn't look away. My heart started to race and my girly parts clenched. He winked and then started his next song, completely unfazed by me. How stereotypical could I flippin' be? One look from a hot rock star and my world tilts? Absolutely not. I will not be *that* girl. Amy and I were supposed to party with Luke tonight, which meant I'd most likely be partying with Dash as well. I won't embarrass myself or Luke. I. Will. Not. I refused to look at Dash while he sang the next song; it was the principle of it.

Amy elbowed me in the ribs, "Uh, Lex? Dash is staring at you."

In order to keep myself from ogling him, I'd taken up counting the number of topless women in the crowd. FYI: I got to twenty without even having to search that hard. I looked back in Dash's direction. Yep, he was staring. I smiled. I couldn't help it. He smiled back. His smile was one of those panty-dropping megawatt smiles—the kind that makes you feel like you are the only person in the world that could elicit that particular smile, even though you know logically many a girl have been lured in with it.

Dash kept his eyes on mine, but spoke into his microphone. "Uh, guys? There is a sexy brunette standing over here to my right. Does she belong to one of y'all? Please tell me she doesn't." He winked at me again. Amy had a death grip on my arm.

Luke stood up and peered over his drums trying to see into the shadows to where we were standing. "Is she standing next to a blonde chick with big blue eyes that's drooling even though she's clearly wearing a wedding ring?" The crowd laughed and so did Amy.

Dash chuckled, "As a matter of fact, yes she is."

Luke nodded and sat back down. "That's my friend Lexi."

Dash's smile grew. "Well isn't that just the best thing I've heard all night. So, Lexi…are you enjoying the show?"

I couldn't help but laugh at this situation. A rock god was flirting with me over the sound system in a sold-out stadium. I nodded my head yes.

"Good. Can I get you anything? This is officially our first date by the way."

I bit down on my lip, contemplating how to play this. I could laugh him off and say no…or…I could have the time of my life with a rock star. I tipped my hand back towards my mouth, indicating I wanted a drink.

"Could someone please get my girl a drink?" Dash turned back towards the crowd. "Sorry about that folks but I've been staring at her since the show started." He led into the next song; the crowd sang every word right along with him.

Some guy walked over and handed each of us a beer. Amy turned to me. "Holy shit, Lex. You have to do him. You have to. On behalf of every married woman out there, you have to sleep with Dash Conner."

"On behalf of *every* married woman, Ams? Or on behalf of you?" I took a long pull of my beer. Amy married her college sweetheart and even though she was in fact drooling, they were deliriously happy together.

"Come on, Lexi. One night with a sexy rock god. Who turns that down?"

"I do. I'm too old for one night stands, rock god or not."

"Will you at least make out with him?"

"Oh yeah, for sure. I'm responsible, not stupid." We both laughed and turned our attention back to the show. It was easy to get swept up in the music; they were mesmerizing. After a couple more songs, Dash looked back over at me.

"How you doing, Kitten? Need another drink?" I held my bottle upside down, frowning, showing him it was empty and nodded. Dash smiled. "Someone will bring you a new drink. Show's almost over, sweetheart." He looked away. I suddenly felt lonely without his eyes on me.

Amy jumped up and down next to me. "Holy ball sack! You are going to mess around with the hottest man on the planet. I *will* live vicariously through you."

I downed half my new beer in a couple swallows. "Amy, calm down. I'm sure once he realizes that I'm not going to just jump in his bed, he'll go find someone else to play with. We came here to hang with Lukey. That's what I want to do."

A couple of songs later the show ended. The band thanked their fans and came jogging off the stage right towards us. Luke reached us first. He pulled Amy and I both in for a hug. "I'm so hyped you two are here! Are y'all ready to party with some rock stars?" Luke laughed with his arms slung around our shoulders. "Let me introduce you to the band." He used the hand around Amy to point at their bassist—dirty blond hair, piercing blue eyes, perfect olive skin, and a smile that didn't quite displace the sadness in his eyes. "This is Smith James. He's from New Orleans. His accent makes panties melt so be careful." Next he motioned to a tall dark-haired sex-on-a-stick wearing an almost inappropriately tight t-shirt and a wide, cocky grin. "Jacks Cole—don't let his shirts fool you, he isn't gay." And last, all eyes fell on Dash, rock god extraordinaire. "Dash Conner, lead singer and the man hitting on Lexi in front of a sold-out stadium crowd."

Dash took my hand and tried to pull me away from Luke. Luke held on tight; Dash pulled harder. I was like the rope in a game of tug-o-war. I looked up at Luke, smiling. "It's okay, Lukey, it's not like he's going to kidnap me." Dash pulled again and this time Luke let go.

Dash grinned, "First of all, Lukey? That nickname will be revisited, a lot. Second of all, don't be so sure, Kitten."

Chapter Two

Dash

I did want to kidnap her. I wanted to lock her in my bedroom and make her scream my name for hours on end. I wanted to lick her whole body, from head to toe. Lexi captivated my attention from the second she stepped up to the side of the stage. Her brunette hair fell down her back in easy waves. Her body was straight sin, thin but curvy in all the right places. Now that I was close to her, I could see her eyes were the greenest green I'd ever seen. The best part about Lexi though? Her smile. It was constantly mischievous, like she knew a secret that no one else knew. "So, *Lukey*, what did you have in mind for these beautiful girls tonight? Dancing? Shots? Strip club?"

Lexi threw her head back and laughed. "Oh no, no strip clubs. I haven't recovered from my last stripper encounter."

My gut clenched. For some reason, my mind didn't like the idea of male strippers rubbing themselves all over my new little Kitten. "Do I even want to know? Lap dance gone wrong?"

This time it was Amy's turn to laugh. She pointed at Luke. "You could say that."

Luke immediately put his hand over Amy's mouth. "No way, Ams. You promised you would never ever tell this story. You pinky swore."

Amy held her hands up in surrender. "You are right, Lukey. I did promise. But…Lexi didn't."

While we were talking we had made our way to our large dressing room at the back of the venue. I opened the door and motioned for everyone to go in. There was a stocked bar and plenty of room to party, at least until they kicked us out. Before I shut the door I leaned out to talk to our security guy. "No 'fans' tonight, Chase. Keep them away from here and keep them off the bus."

"Uh, boss, the ones you and Smith picked earlier are already on the bus waiting."

"Get rid of them." I shut the door and turned around to find Lexi looking at me, eyes questioning. I winked. "Just making sure we're all safe from the crazies."

Lexi shook her head and put her hand on Luke's shoulder bringing his forehead to rest against hers. I was oddly jealous of their closeness. "I'm sorry, Lukey, but Amy is right. I never made any promise to keep my mouth shut."

Luke threw his hands in the air. "Are you kidding me, Lex?! I couldn't make you promise. You had your head buried in the toilet puking all freaking night."

Lexi shrugged and sat down in one of the armchairs set up for us. "So, Amy and I decided that we were going to take Luke to his first strip club for his twenty-first birthday—"

I held up my hand. "Wait, you're first strip club experience was with your sister and you were already twenty-one? Wow, haven't heard the whole story and already I'm ashamed of you, man."

Luke rolled his eyes. "Number one, don't tell me you aren't jealous as hell that I was with two beautiful girls at a strip club. One of them isn't a blood relation." He winked at me and Amy swatted his arm. "Number two, where we grew up there weren't any strip clubs. It wasn't until I went to visit Lexi and Amy at school that I was even within driving distance of one."

Lexi waved at the air with her hands. "Y'all stop interrupting my story. Okay the three of us go to this strip club. By the time we get there we're already pretty drunk. Amy ends up taking pole-dancing lessons from a fifty-year-old stripper named Betty, no joke. So it's just me and Luke sitting there watching the...show. I buy him a lap dance, we go into the back room, and long story short Luke ends up...liking it a little tooooooo much."

Jacks and Smith cracked up. The idea of Luke blowing his load from a simple lap dance made them laugh so hard they started crying. Amy was giggling and Lexi was biting her lip to keep from smiling too big. But the reaction I noticed the most? Luke's. He wasn't laughing; he wasn't even smiling. He looked tormented, broken hearted, and he was staring right at Lexi. I narrowed my eyes. "Lexi, you were there? You actually watched this poor boy get his first lap dance."

Lexi snorted, "I did. I didn't want to be left alone out there on the main floor."

I nodded, realization making me feel bad for the guy. He didn't blow his load from the lap dance. He came from watching Lexi, while he got a lap dance. Luke liked her. He wanted her. Or at least he had at one time. Well shit.

Chapter Three

Lexi

We stayed in the dressing room drinking and telling story after story of youth gone wrong. Dash had gone from sitting across the room from me to sitting on the floor in front of me, leaning back against the chair. After my third shot of Fireball, I had let him put my legs on either side of his body. After my fifth? I let him start to rub his hands up and down my legs. When Jacks set up another round of shots Luke grabbed mine before he could hand it to me. "Oh no, no more Fireball for Lexi. Whiskey makes her too damn pleasing."

I laughed and held my hands up in surrender. "Lukey is right. No more Fireball. I'll take a beer though."

Smith leaned down and opened the mini fridge he was sitting on. "No beer in here. We have some on the bus. They are going to politely ask us to leave this room soon anyway."

We filed out of the room and headed towards the back parking lot and the guys' bus. I figured it would be opulent, but wow. It was huge, the size of a studio apartment. It was all granite counter tops and lush leather furniture. A girl could get used to this. I sat down on the couch next to Amy, who was looking a little tired. Amy was an elementary school teacher. She used to be able to party with the best of us, but now she went to bed early every night. The excitement of the show, drinking, and still being up at one o'clock in the morning was no doubt catching up with her. She closed her eyes and leaned her head against my shoulder. Luke came and lifted her into his arms. "Come on, Ams. You can sleep in my bed. I'll take the couch."

She yawned. "No. I'm not tired, really. I never get to see you. We should catch a cab back to Lexi's soon anyway."

Luke kissed her forehead. "No worries, Ams, we don't pull out of here until ten tomorrow. You sleep. We'll have breakfast together." There was no more argument out of her.

Smith stretched his arms over his head. "Not to sound like a giant dick, but I gotta go find some strange or I'll never be able to fall asleep tonight." He held his hand out to me. "It was really great to meet you, Lexi. I'll see you in the morning?"

I smiled as I took his hand. "Yes, sir." He went down the steps and before the door shut I heard him call out to a guy named Chase. I could have sworn I heard him say, "Where'd you put that chick?"

Jacks chuckled as he stood. "I'm going to uh…go with Smith. Don't think I'm a jerk, okay?"

I shook my head. "No judgment here, buddy. Have fun." After Jacks left, Luke walked back into the room and sat down next to me. It was just he, I, and Dash left.

Luke cleared his throat. "Amy is in my bunk. There is an extra one right above her. You can stay there. I have clothes if you want to change. I'll just sleep on the couch."

Dash stretched his arms above his head, revealing the most delicious six-pack I'd ever seen. He had tattoos on his abs too, gnarly looking music notes. I wanted to trace them with my tongue. Whoa, I really did drink too much whiskey. "Nah man, you take the bedroom tonight. I'll crash on the couch. I'm not ready for bed anyway. I think I'll stay up and write some."

Luke's eyebrows rose to his hairline. "Really? You aren't going out?" Watching them volley back and forth was fun. It was like watching two beautiful lions circle a kill, each striving for dominance.

"Not tonight man."

Luke threaded his fingers through mine. "You ready for bed, Lex? I can tuck you in, just like old times."

I leaned my head back against the couch. I knew what I should do. I should take Luke up on his offer; he'd give me jammies, tuck me in, kiss my forehead and walk away. It's what he'd always done…well except for that once. But I wasn't ready for bed, and I wasn't craving safe and predictable. I wanted the sexy rock god that had been undressing me with his eyes all night. I wanted his dark piercing gaze to stay on me. I wanted his lips on mine and his hands all over my body. "You know, I think I might stay up for a bit. It's not that late…and I have no plans tomorrow."

Luke stood and let out a deep breath. "Sure, yeah. I'll just be at the end of the hall. If you need anything, anything at all." He leaned forward, putting his hands on my cheeks, kissing my forehead. "Sweet dreams, my Little Lex." I smiled at the nickname. When I first met him, I called him Little Luke, because he was Amy's little brother, not because there was anything little about him. He wasn't

18

even that much younger than us, he was twenty-four to our twenty-seven. He'd countered "Little Luke" with "Little Lex." After he disappeared down the hall and we heard the door click shut, Dash came over and sat next to me on the couch. He picked up the remote and turned on the large flat screen TV mounted on the wall opposite us.

"What do you want to watch, Kitten? Porn okay?"

I rolled my eyes at the nickname, not because it was bothering me, but because I was secretly starting to love it. Which made me feel like a stupid naïve girl. "No porn, please. I can't take it seriously. The storylines are horrible."

He looked me, confused. "What story lines?"

I laughed. "Nice. I thought you wanted to write anyway?"

Dash took my hand in his. "I do. I want to do *you* more though...so...no porn?"

"For real? 'I want to do you more?' Gross. Try harder." I flicked his wrist with my free hand. The word "flawed" was scrawled down his forearm in large letters.

He smiled this cute little crooked smile. "So you're saying there's a chance?"

I giggled. Dash was charming and sexy; I didn't want to tell him no. "Look, let me just lay it all out for you. I'm not a groupie. I'm not into one-night stands. I won't have sex with you. So if that's what you're looking for tonight, you might as well have followed Jacks and Smith out the door to the ass you already had lined up." I held my hand up when he tried to argue that point. "I'm not stupid, Dash. But if you want to hang out—get to know each other a little more—I'd like that."

"Can we at least make out?"

I bit my lip to keep from smiling. "Sure."

Chapter Four

Dash

Sure? She agreed to make out with me...just not fuck me. Oh well, one step at a time I suppose. That wasn't usually my style, but Lexi was different from girls I usually went for. She was honest, direct; she didn't seem to give two shits that I was rich and famous. It felt like when she looked at me, she saw me. She saw everything; she was so observant. Except when it came to Luke. Either she knew he loved her and she ignored it, or she was clueless when it came to him. I watched them together. I watched for signs that she was into him, that I should back off. But I saw none. Lexi cared about Luke, no doubt about it. But she didn't look at him with lust in her eyes. "So...now? Or...?"

She threw her head back and laughed. I liked her laugh. It was so vibrant and carefree. "Just like that? I mean, no wooing me or anything?"

"Wooing you? I haven't 'wooed' a chick since before my first record deal." I wasn't exaggerating. Once we signed on the dotted line, girls pretty much started throwing themselves at us.

"Give it shot. Make me *want* to kiss you. You said this was our first date right? Woo me." She smiled, and in that instant, I wanted to.

I narrowed my eyes, pursed my lips like I was thinking really hard about what to do to make her want me to kiss her. I reached over the side of the couch and pulled out Smith's guitar. "Come sit on my lap." Lexi gave me what can only be described as a withering look. I rolled my eyes. "This is me wooing. Now will you please come sit on my lap?"

She was trying not to smile—she bit her lip when she was trying to appear unaffected by something. That much I'd learned tonight. Lexi crawled into my lap. She was so damn tiny. She could sit cross-legged and there was still plenty of room for me to balance the guitar on her legs and reach it well enough to play. "Pick a song, any song."

She looked over her shoulder at me. Her mouth was so close it would only take me inches to touch my lips to hers. "Really?"

"Really."

Lexi turned back around, tapping her chin in contemplation. "'Into the Mystic,' Van Morrison."

I wanted to fist bump the air. Not only could I play this song in my sleep, but it was one of my favorites. Van Morrison always seemed to soothe me, calm my nerves. "Good choice, Kitten." I strummed the first few chords and put my mouth close to her ear as I began to sing, *"We were born before the wind, also younger than the sun…"* As I sang, Lexi closed her eyes. I could literally feel her body melting into mine. Huh, turns out I knew how to woo a girl after all. I finished the song and placed my hand on the instrument, quieting the final notes. Pulling her hair off her neck, I leaned forward and kissed her. Softly. The little moan that escaped her mouth made my eyes roll back in my head. "Careful, Kitten," I kissed her again, "Too many moans like that and I'll go from romantic to raunchy real quick." I felt her laughter more than I heard it. "Look at me, Lexi."

I put the guitar on the couch next to us and she turned around in my lap. I guided her hips until she was straddling me. I cupped her face in my hands. "What is it about you? You make me want to be better, be different."

She closed her eyes and smiled. "I'm thoroughly wooed. Now kiss me."

"Yes ma'am." I kissed her. I kissed her like a man kissing a woman, not like a rock star kissing an easy lay. I paid attention; I noticed what made her shiver, what made her slowly grind her body against mine. She liked it when I tugged her hair, when I nipped her lower lip. We made out on the couch for what felt like hours. Just kissing and touching. I didn't push her and she didn't hold me back. It was perfection and I—

"Whoa, sorry, didn't mean to interrupt."

Damn. I pulled back and opened my eyes. The dim light from the room was almost too much. That's how long I had been lost in Lexi. Jacks was back, looking thoroughly fucked. Oddly enough, I wasn't jealous. "Where's Smith?"

"He's right behind me. Don't worry. I didn't leave him. Wouldn't make that mistake twice." Jacks rolled his eyes, grabbed a bottle of water and then lay on the floor. His long body was almost too big for the small space. "So, you two seem to be getting along."

Lexi climbed off my lap. "Did you find what you were looking for?"

I grinned at her tone, playful and curious. I reached for her tanned legs and pulled them into my lap. The little shorts she was wearing would be my undoing. I began to rub her exposed skin. "Well, Jacks, did you?"

Jacks put his hands behind his head, "Of course I did. Did you?"

I looked over at Lexi, wanting to see her reaction to Jacks's question. He meant no harm by it, but would she get all pissy with what he was implying?

She threw a pillow at his head and laughed. "I did...Dash might still be looking for more."

I shook my head. "Only if you're the one offering, Kitten." She bit her lower lip again.

Smith walked in, closing and locking the door behind him. "That was the worst head I've ever had. Ever." He stopped short when he saw Lexi was still up with us. "Oh, uh, I'm sorry. I thought— Sorry, Lexi."

She just laughed. "No worries, buddy. Sorry you had bad head, nothing worse than that, right?"

Smith stuck out his lower lip and sat on the floor next to Lexi. "No, there really isn't." He laid his head on the couch, rubbing his dirty blond hair against her hand like a dog.

She rolled her eyes and started rubbing his head, "Aw poor little rock star."

This girl was perfect. She was sexy and beautiful, nothing offended her, she liked Van Morrison...I mean, holy hell. I got to my feet and reached for her hand.

"Come on, Kitten, bed time."

"Noooooooooo! Let her rub my head some more. I've had a bad night, man."

I flicked Smith on the forehead. "Suck it up, sailor. You and I both know that bad head is better than no head. I don't feel bad for you. We're going to bed."

Jacks snickered. "Together? Better keep it down. You know how bitchy Luke gets when other people's sex wakes him up. He threw my box of condoms out the window last time I made that mistake."

Chapter Five

Lexi

I was letting this gorgeous man lead me down the hall, to a bed that he wanted to share? I had nearly given in while we were making out on the couch. Jacks walked in just in time. Would I be able to say no when we were lying all tangled together and alone?

Dash opened a drawer from a dresser built into the hallway. "Jacks's clothes would no doubt fit you better, but the idea of seeing you in his t-shirt makes me see red. Here is one of mine. I'd give you bottoms to wear…but I just really don't wanna." He smiled that cute crooked smile, the one that made my knees feel weak.

I took the clothes and went into the bathroom to change. It was larger than I expected it to be, with a full size shower and double vanity. Man, these guys had some money. I wondered if they owned this bus or rented it for the tour. When I came out Dash was leaning against the wall, arms crossed, brow furrowed. "What's with the face?"

He shrugged. "Just wondering if I was going to be able to sleep next to you without trying to get in your pants."

I leaned against the opposite wall, mirroring his posture. "And?"

Dash straightened and took my hand, pulling me against his chest. "It'll be hard. But I'll do it, because I'm not ready to let you go." He leaned down and placed a soft, chaste kiss on my lips.

Wow. That was definitely not the response I thought I'd get. I was expecting something cocky or sarcastic or even a proposition. Sweet honesty was a shock, one more defense down. "All right, where are we sleeping, Casanova?"

Dash reached above my head and pulled back a curtain revealing a twin size bed. It looked comfy enough, with nice sized pillows and a fluffy down comforter. But it was small, and it was going to be a hella tight fit. Dash had his self-control all straightened out, but what about mine? "That's a really small bed."

Dash patted the mattress, gesturing for me to climb in first. "We'll fit, trust me. We'll just have to spoon." I slapped his hand away when he tried to help me up by palming my ass.

I climbed in and turned on my side facing him. "I take it you know we'll fit from experience. So the big bad rocker likes to cuddle?"

He settled his head on the pillow and placed his hand on my hip. "I knew that we'd fit because I never let girls stay the night when I'm in one of the bunks. This big bad rocker doesn't cuddle, ever."

I ran my fingers down his arm, tracing the words "every saint has a past and every sinner has a future." "What makes me special?"

Dash reached around my hip and grabbed my ass, bringing his body closer to mine. "Everything? Nothing? I wish I knew. But you are, you know, special." Call me naïve, but something in his eyes made me believe him. He fused his mouth to mine and our tongues danced to their own song. His hands were everywhere and I fucking loved it. I fisted mine in his hair and guided his mouth to my neck. On his own accord he moved even lower and took my breast in his mouth. Everything he did to me felt so good, so fucking perfect. I felt him pull back and when I opened my eyes, he was staring at me. The desire in his gaze made my breath hitch.

"We need to stop. I would love to keep kissing you, but we need to stop. I want you too much." He rested his forehead against mine. "Turn around." I did as I was told and was rewarded when his body pressed against mine. Every part of him was holding every part of me. How was I supposed to walk away from this in the morning? We had only made out, and I knew I would dream about him every night for the next year. He ruined me for any other man. I had never felt so desired, so wanted, so special. Dash's hand snaked its way around my hips until his bare hand was resting on my stomach and then he whispered, "Good night, Kitten."

Chapter Six

Dash

Her breathing had evened out, she was asleep, and I was still wide-awake. I ran my fingers lightly down her body, rubbing her bare legs from calf to hip. I don't know where the will power to stop came from, nor did I know where the desire to simply sleep next to this girl came from. Maybe the same place? I loved that she had crawled into bed wearing my t-shirt and some cute boy shorts panties. I loved that she didn't try to cover up or hide herself from me. Lexi was comfortable in her own skin, confident, and it was so damn sexy. I hadn't slept next to a girl like this since I was a kid. It was either drunken sex and then passed out cold, or drunken sex and me kicking a girl off the bus. I hadn't lied; I didn't do overnights unless I was in the big bed in the back of the bus. I didn't cuddle. I was a fucking rock star. Lexi shifted in her sleep. Her ass rubbed against my dick. Holy hell it was going to be long night.

***

I woke up with my body plastered over Lexi's. We weren't just cuddling; I was wrapped around her like a fucking anaconda. I brushed a piece of hair off her face and kissed her nose. "Wake up, Kitten." She swatted at me and let out an angry groan. "Whoa, I take it you aren't a morning person?" I ran my finger across her jaw.

She repeated the swat and groan maneuver, then turned and faced the wall. She wiggled her sexy little body back against mine and mumbled, "What time is it? Why are you awake?"

I checked my watch and then buried my face in her hair, inhaling deeply. "It's six-thirty, and I'm awake because I have a ragging case of blue balls." I hissed when she rubbed her ass against me. "That's not nice, Kitten. I said I'd behave last night. I didn't say anything about this morning."

She flipped back over, burying her head under my chin. "If I promise to play nice will you let me go back to sleep?"

"Maybe..." How nice was she talking? My breath caught in my chest when I felt her hand slide between our bodies and grip my cock. "Kitten? What are you doing?"

She wrapped her hand around me tighter, stroking from base to tip. "Playing nice." At some point during the night I'd taken off my shirt, and thank God I had because now she was kissing and nibbling my collarbone. She continued to work me with her hand, and it felt fucking fantastic. I couldn't even remember the last time a chick had given me a hand job…maybe like freshman year of high school? My pulse quickened and my balls started to throb; holy hell, I was going to come any second. "Lexi…I…oh God…wait—"

She turned her face up and kissed my chin, licked my ear and then whispered, "It's okay. I want you to. Please, Dash." And then she let out one of her little moans, like jacking me turned her on. That was my undoing. I came all over her hands and my stomach.

I threw an arm over my face and chuckled, "Damn, Lex, what did you do to me? How did you make a hand job so erotic?"

I felt her shrug. "Motivation, I guess. Can I go back to sleep now?"

I kissed the top of her head and grabbed the t-shirt I had taken off, cleaning us both up. "Sure, Kitten, go back to sleep." I snuggled up next to her, tucking her body against mine. And this time, I fell asleep before she did.

***

When I woke up again it was to the sound of people. I couldn't tell what time it was; the curtains that separated the bunks from the hallway were dark and thick. I would check my watch but Lexi was lying on that arm. I reached behind me and cracked the curtain. I was met with Amy's smiling face.

"Morning, Dash! You haven't seen my best friend Lexi have you?" She winked.

I looked past her, trying to tell if everyone else was up, if they had noticed that I wasn't asleep on the couch like I said I would be. And by everyone else, I meant Luke. I looked back at Amy.

"Smith is in the shower, Jacks is brushing his teeth in the kitchen, and Luke is still in bed. You know him, he likes his sleep."

I looked over at Lexi and smiled. "He isn't the only one apparently."

Amy laughed, "You didn't try to wake her before seven did you?"

"I did."

"Did she hit you?"

I smiled. "Twice."

Amy looked over at the bedroom door and then back to me, her smile falling slightly. "I wanted to wake up Lexi before I got Luke up." She shrugged. "I mean, I just…I thought it would be easier that way. He can get pretty protective over Lex and—"

I interrupted her. "Hey, no worries. I understand. I'll get her up." She just nodded and headed towards the living room, not where Luke was sleeping.

I closed the curtain and nuzzled Lexi's ear. No joke, nuzzled. What the hell was happening to me? "Kitten, it really is time to get up now okay? It's time for breakfast. Everyone's awake."

Lexi stretched her arms and yawned, she sat up, hit her head on the low ceiling and then lay back down. "Balls."

I tried not to laugh, really I did. But between her scowl and her use of "balls" as a cuss word, I couldn't help it. "Aw, Kitten, are you okay?" I rubbed her head.

"I'm fine. Where are my shorts?"

I reached down to the foot of the bed and handed her clothes to her. "I don't think there is enough material there for those to actually be considered shorts."

She shot me a glare. "I didn't hear you complaining about my shorts last night when you couldn't keep your hands off my legs."

I grinned. "I wasn't complaining now. Just making an observation. You sure are feisty in the morning." I watched shamelessly as she got dressed. She left my shirt on instead of changing into hers. I kept my immense pleasure about it to myself. She pulled her long hair into a messy bun at the top of her head. She looked effortlessly beautiful. "All right, Kitten, I'm going to go shower all the dried come off my stomach. Thanks for that by the way. The lengths you'll go to in order to get another two hours of sleep are astounding."

Lexi kept her eyes locked with mine; a slow sexy smile came over her face. She climbed on top of me, rubbing her core against my dick. She closed her eyes, threw her head back and let out one of those moans that I'd come to love so much. Then she smacked me on the stomach and hopped out of the bunk. I think she's my soul mate.

Chapter Seven

Lexi

If anyone noticed that I'd spent the night in the same bunk as Dash, no one said anything. And by anyone, I meant Luke. It's not like either of us was hiding it. Dash found any and all excuses to touch me during breakfast and I was wearing his shirt. But I didn't want a lecture from Luke. We'd both behaved and I didn't want to have to explain everything to him. We'd all gone to breakfast at one of my favorite Mexican food places. It was a hole in the wall, but that's what made it good. Now we were all sitting around the bus, trying to put off the moment when Amy and I had to leave.

Luke put his arm around Amy's shoulder. "Y'all stay. Ride to Houston with us and I'll fly you home on Monday. Plllllease. I haven't seen you guys in months."

Amy cocked her head to the side, contemplating. I knew she would move heaven and earth if it meant she got to spend even a little more time with her baby brother. "You sure you want your sisters here two nights in a row? Aren't we messing up your game?" Amy and I both smiled at that. Luke was gorgeous, but kind. If he wanted to he could have run outside, grabbed a girl, nailed her against the bus and been back twenty minutes later. But that wasn't Luke. He didn't do easy.

Jacks put his arm around my waist pulling me against his side. "What about you, Lexi? Think you can handle another night with a group of rock stars?"

Dash walked in and saw me leaning on Jacks, smiling up at him. How could I not? He was adorable in his tiny t-shirt. Dash stalked across the room and took my hand, pulling me away from his band mate. Jacks laughed.

"If Amy wants to stay, then I'll stay on until Houston." I looked over at her, my eyebrows raised in question.

"Let me just go call Parker. And I'll have to call work. Man, Lex, I wish I had your freedom." Amy pulled out her phone and stepped into the bathroom. Her husband Parker absolutely adored Luke. He would have no problems with Amy wanting to stay with her brother. I assumed she needed privacy to call and leave a fake sick message for work.

Dash smiled—the sex god smile, not the adorable one I loved. "What is it that you do, Kitten. How are you so free?"

"I'm a freelance photographer."

"Are you any good?"

I stood on tiptoe and whispered in his ear, "You know I'm good," before spinning out of his grasp.

Luke came up and placed his chin on my shoulder. "She's amazing."

Dash narrowed his eyes at Luke. "Why does everyone keep touching her? Stop touching her."

I laughed. Was the rocker jealous? "I'm right here and if I want Luke to stop touching me, I'll ask him to." Luke rubbed his chin stubble across my neck taunting Dash.

Dash cocked his head. "You know, we're looking for someone to photograph the tour for our next album. Can I see some of your work?"

"You may…." I was proud and passionate as hell about my work. I was good and I knew it. Touring with The Devil's Share would be a huge opportunity for me, my art would be seen by millions, but I was wary. Touring with the guys meant more time with Dash and I knew myself—I'd give in and sleep with him. And I doubted it would end in a happily ever after. Plus, I'd toured with a band before, and that had turned out to be a nightmare.

Luke pulled out his phone and handed it to Dash. "The folder marked 'Lex.' Those are all pictures she did of me and my old band." I heard the sadness in Luke's voice when he mentioned his first band. I knew he missed the guys he grew up with, the guys he learned to play with. He rarely talked about them. I wondered if The Devil's Share crew even knew what Luke had gone through, knew the kind of guy he was. He was hands down the most amazing man I'd ever known.

Dash scrolled through the pictures. "These are really good, Lexi. Like real, real good. I'm impressed. And I want you."

I snorted, "I think we already established that you *want* me."

Dash called over his shoulder, "Y'all come over here and look at these pictures." He passed Luke's phone around, the guys all taking a turn to scroll through my work.

Smith looked up. "These are the exact kind of pictures we wanted for our new album. No joke, Lexi. You have to say yes."

I bit my lip to keep from smiling. It was hella flattering to have this group of very talented artists appreciate my work. The pictures were mostly candid shots I took when the band hadn't been looking. Shots of them with their heads down practicing, or them asleep on the couch piled next to each other. The pictures I took of Luke's old band were raw, and full of contrast. I used filters to make the guys seem dark and grungy. Little did I know, weeks later I wouldn't even need filters to make the band look that way. All the pictures tugged at my heartstrings. That little tour I went on with them was the beginning of the end. It wasn't a stadium tour by any means, but they were gaining popularity and had a strong following. The pictures pretty much chronicled their decent into sex drugs and rock-n-roll. Well, all of them except for Luke. He told me one night after way too many Van Morrison songs and way too much whiskey that I saved him. That my being on the tour with him kept him grounded and home at night. But I knew that wasn't the case. I knew that it was his heart that kept him clean, his pure love for the music. He was a good man, through and through. He tried to kiss me that night. I hadn't let him.

I was jerked back from my trip down memory lane when Dash rudely snapped his fingers in front of my face. "Focus, Kitten. What do you say? We'll pay you an ungodly amount of money. And I promise to make you very happy every night."

"Oh yeah? You're going to bake me fresh cookies and watch *The Original's* with me?"

Luke chuckled.

Dash pursed his lips, "What?"

"Making me happy every night. That's what you said, right? I assumed that by 'make me happy' you meant cookies and vampire dramas. What else could you possibly mean?" I winked.

Dash narrowed his eyes and shook his head before shooting me the crooked grin.

Smith raised his hand. "Uh, if you say yes, I'll bake."

"And I'll watch whatever *The Originals* is with you anytime you like." Jacks put one hand on my shoulder and flipped Dash off with the other.

"What do you say, Lex? You already know that I'll do whatever it takes to keep you with me." Luke's smile turned sad, and his eyes became very puppy dog like. "You know I need you."

Ass wipe. He knew those sweet words in that sad tone would be my undoing. He also knew how big this would end up being for my career. "Fine, I'll do it. One condition though…" I smiled at Luke. "And you know what it is…."

Luke started to shake his head. "No. No way, Lexi. Dagger isn't coming."

I shrugged, "No Dagger, no me."

Luke stomped his foot like a petulant child. "Come on, Lex. Let Amy and Parker watch him."

Amy walked back into the room. "Let Amy and Parker watch who? Dagger? No. He ate my couch last time we watched him. Wait. Why do you need a dog sitter?"

Dash put both his hands on my shoulders, pulling me back against him and this time I stayed. "Kitten here has agreed to tour with us and be our onsite photographer. And of course your little dog can come."

Amy started jumping up and down and clapping her hands. Then she hit me. "I am so damn jealous!"

***

Amy agreed to run home with me so I could pack up all my stuff and get back on the bus before we left for Houston. I was so glad that we had one more night all together before Amy had to go back to Dallas. If I could keep her with me for the whole tour, I would in heartbeat. We spent so much time together; I knew I'd miss her. But hey, I got Luke. "Ams?"

She was busy sliding everything from my bathroom counter into a bag. I guess that was one way of speed packing. Although I doubted I'd need three bottles of perfume on tour. "Yeah?"

"Do you think Luke would be mad at me if I ended up hooking up with Dash while we were on the road?"

She brought the bag into my room and set it down on my bed. "I don't think he'd be *mad*. I think he'd worry. Why? You planning on having a hot love affair with Dash Conner? Or did you already start one last night?"

I groaned and flopped down next to my now over-packed bathroom bag. "We didn't have sex. We just made out a little. And spooned. It was perfect and he was…surprisingly sweet. I just have a feeling that being in such close proximity to him for so long…it'll end up less sweet and more steamy."

Amy sat down next to me. "Lex this is a once in a lifetime opportunity. Take pictures, drink too much, dance, sing, fuck a rock star. Live it up."

I shook my head. "Sometimes I wonder how in the world you ended up as an elementary school teacher."

"Me too. And by the way, the correct term is steamier, not more steamy."

Chapter Eight

Lexi

"What the hell is that?" Jacks jumped up on the couch as I boarded the bus with Amy and my dog.

I laughed, "Jacks, meet Dagger."

"That is not a dog, that is a small horse. Good God, Lexi, what kind of dog is he?"

Jacks was still standing on the couch. I stifled another laugh as I answered, "He is a mutt…but mostly he's pit bull." I loved Dagger more that life itself. He was the sweetest, most wonderfully goofy, loving dog ever. "I know he looks kind of intimidating, but I promise, if you just give him a chance you'll love him."

Smith came up the stairs and stepped around us. He stopped so fast when he saw Dagger he lost his footing. "Holy hell."

Jacks nodded. "Smith, this is Dagger. Lexi's 'little dog' and our new tour mascot."

I put my bag down and took Dagger's leash off. I sat down on the couch next to Jacks. Dagger immediately followed and parked it on the floor at my feet, leaning all of his almost hundred pound weight against my leg. I scratched behind his ear and kissed his soft gray face, well his whole body was gray really. Solid gray with beautiful blue eyes. "Stop being such babies. He's just a dog. Now come pet him and say hello."

Amy giggled from the armchair across the room. Jacks sat down next to me, but kept his feet on the couch. He slowly reached out and patted Dagger's head. Smith came and sat on the other side of me and did the same. Fast-forward ten minutes? Dagger was stretched out across all three of our laps, snoring. A cool breeze signaled that the door had just opened, seconds later Luke came up the steps. "Ah, Dagger. How I've missed you, buddy." At the sound of his name Dagger jumped up off our laps and made it to Luke in one bounding leap. Luke fell on the floor and Dagger assaulted him with kisses. "Worst behaved dog in the history of the world."

I wrinkled my nose. "He isn't bad. He's just aggressive with his affection."

Smith chuckled, "Spoken like a true mother, blind to her child's imperfections."

I scoffed, "I don't know what you're talking about. He has no imperfections."

Dagger got up and made a beeline for the door when he heard it open again. *That must be Dash.* I braced myself for his reaction. Dash simply planted his feet and held his hand out towards Dagger.

"Sit." And my dog sat.

Luke stood up and threw his hands in the air. "How in the fuck did you do that? That dog doesn't listen to anybody. Ever. Do you have any idea how many times I've begged that dog to sit the hell down?" Luke cocked his head. "Are you like a dog whisper?"

Dash laughed as he reached down and petted Dagger before kissing his cheek, just like I had. *Damn, a sexy man that likes my dog? There go more defenses.* "I'm good with animals. And women." He winked at me.

***

The bus had just taken off, heading towards the guys' next venue. Amy had gone to take a nap; she was a little hung over. Smith was sitting in a recliner with a guitar in his lap and a pencil in his teeth. Every once in a while he would jot some stuff down in the spiral notebook balanced on the arm of the chair. His hair looked almost gold when the sun's rays would hit it through the window. The lighting was perfect. I snapped a few pictures. Dash was sitting on the couch next to me. He had his phone in his hands; his fingers were flying a mile a minute. I assumed he was answering emails. I guess he could be sexting. I hoped he wasn't sexting.

Jacks was sitting cross-legged on the floor, leaning his back against Dagger's massive body as he played some war game on the Xbox. "How did you come up with the name Dagger? I mean, it's badass, but were did it come from?"

I smiled. "His nickname is Dags. Get it?"

Jacks shook his head, "Nope."

I rolled my eyes. "Say it out loud."

"Dags?"

Smith smiled. "Do you like Dags?"

Dash laughed, "*Snatch*? You got your giant pit bull's name from the movie *Snatch*?"

I nodded. "I did. I love that movie. And tell me that's not the coolest name for a dog, like ever?"

He grinned and pulled my legs into his lap. "It is the coolest name ever, and you are officially the coolest chick, ever."

Luke came from the back room, grabbing us all beers on the way. "It's a good thing y'all got it. I've seen Lexi refuse to be friends with people before because they didn't get his name. She uses it to 'weed out' boring people." He handed out the beers and then plopped down between me and Dash, sitting on my legs. I rolled my eyes and pried them from under his ass. Dash flipped him off.

Chapter Nine

Dash

Luke had been sticking to Lexi's side since she and Dagger had boarded the bus. I didn't know if it was because he knew about our little spooning session or because he just wanted to be near her. Like I did. I hadn't been lying before. I was actually really good with dogs. I always had been. My parents were of the mindset that a house just wasn't a home without at least three dogs. Being on the road and constantly working for the past ten years made it almost impossible for me to own a pet. But if I could have handpicked my perfect dog? I would have picked Dagger. He was a giant gray beast with the kindest eyes. Just one more thing to love about Lexi: her impeccable taste. "Okay, so since Lexi is the only girl on the bus annnnnd she has a hundred pound dog that will be sleeping next to her, she gets the bedroom."

Jacks threw down his controller. "What?! No way. We keep the schedule and Dagger can sleep with whoever sleeps in the bedroom." He leaned back against the dog and rubbed his ears.

Lexi held up her hands. "I don't need special treatment. I don't mind doing the rotation schedule for the bed. HOWEVER, you must always change the sheets. ALWAYS. And Dags sleeps in there with you, he doesn't like to be alone."

Smith took the pencil out of his mouth. "Fine by me, besides, the only reason Dash wants Lexi to get the bedroom is because she'll let him bunk in there with her."

Luke shot up from the couch and turned to glare at me. "What the fuck does that mean?"

Aw hell, I guess he didn't know we shared a bed last night. "Lexi and I bunked together last night. It's not a big deal, nothing happened."

Jacks chuckled, "Looked pretty hot and heavy when I walked in."

I was about to reach across the room and sucker punch him when Lexi threw her water bottle at his head. "Can it, Jacks. Nobody asked you." Ha, this girl had spunk. She barely knew these guys and she was already treating them like the brothers she never wanted.

I turned my attention back to Luke. He was still towering over me, his face red. He looked pissed. "Dash, can I please speak to you? Privately."

I'm not sure how he got those words out when his teeth were clenched together so damn tight. Lexi reached out and grabbed his hand. "Lukey, I love you for caring, but this really isn't any of your business."

Luke straight up ignored her. His eyes never wavered from mine. I glared right back. "Sure, we can talk. Step into my new bedroom." It was a low blow, I know. But he had ignored Lexi and he was starting to irritate me a little. Luke followed me down the hall and into the back bedroom. It was dark in there, and cool from the door being shut and the AC blowing. It was like a little cave. I wanted to bring Lex in here and get hot under the covers. I leaned against the wall, arms crossed, face impassive waiting for Luke to say his piece.

He ran his fingers through his hair and down his face. "What are you doing Dash? Lexi is important to me, man."

"She's important to me too." I was shocked at the words that just spilled from my mouth, shocked at how true they were.

Luke rolled his eyes. "Yeah right. To you all girls are all the same. They are all toys, all disposable. Lexi isn't a groupie. She isn't a whore. You can't toss her out when you're done. Wait. Is that why you wanted to hire her? So you could have on-premise pussy? I'll fucking kill you."

I held my hands up. "Hold the fuck up, dude. First of all, I hired Lex because she is fantastic at what she does." It wasn't lost on me that fantastic was the word I used to describe her hand job skills this morning. "Second of all, I like her, okay? I like her. And nothing happened last night. I want to spend time with her. I want to know her. I won't hurt her, Luke. Do you two…do y'all have a history? Is that what this is about?"

Luke sighed, his shoulders slumping in defeat. "You really like her? You aren't just using her?"

I put my right hand over my heart and raised my left. "I swear, Luke. I'm not using her." I dropped both my hands to my sides. "Are you going to answer my question now? Is there something going on between you two?"

Luke stared at me for a while before dropping his gaze to his shoes. "No. There isn't anything between us. We're friends, family.

I'd die for her though. Make no mistake, man, she means the fucking world to me." He walked out and left me staring after him.

I knew I should go back out and hang with the crew. I knew that it would be wrong to rub the situation in Luke's face when he was obviously upset. But a nap with Lexi was way too tempting. We hadn't been alone together in hours and I just wanted to kiss her so damn bad. I sat down on the bed and called out, "Dagger, come." A few seconds later I heard his massive paws thumping down the hall. He appeared in the doorway and just like I had hoped, Lexi was standing behind him.

"Did you need Dags for something?" She smirked. She knew what I was doing.

"I needed him to bring me you. Come take a nap with me." She looked over her shoulder at me. She bit her lower lip. She was torn. But in the end she shut and locked the door and climbed in bed next to me. Dagger put one foot on the mattress. "Oh no, sir. You sleep on the floor. Down." I snapped and pointed at the ground. He huffed but lay down all the same. I reached down and patted his side, "Good boy, Dags." I lay back and turned to face Lexi.

"Is everything okay? Between you and Luke?" She reached out and ran her finger over my eyebrow. Odd, but soothing.

"Everything is fine. He was just worried about your virtue."

At that she laughed. "Virtue? He should have worried about that long ago. I doubt I have any left at this point."

I scowled. "I'm going to pretend I didn't hear that, Kitten. I'm going to pretend that you have loads of virtue left and that you have just been saving it all this time for me."

She giggled, "Go ahead and pretend all you want babe. It's not like you have any room to talk." I cupped her face in my palms, rubbing my thumb along her lower lip. "What are we doing, Dash?"

I gave her that crooked grin I knew she liked. "I don't know about you but I was thinking about stealing third base." She laughed. I loved making her laugh. I'd never loved making a girl laugh before. I never even put in the effort to be funny. Hell, I rarely put in the effort to learn their names.

"We work together now. I'm on this bus for the next eight weeks straight before we get a break. I just don't—"

I put my hand over her mouth. Any sentence that started with "I just don't" couldn't be good. Unless it ended with "think you should ever stop touching me." "Here's how I look at it, Kitten—we can either spend the next eight weeks skating around each other, trying to ignore this crazy attraction between us or we can have some fun. I can make you laugh all day and moan all night. I like you. I want you. I choose option two."

Lexi was quiet for so long I started to panic. I didn't know what I'd do if she turned me down. I had to have her, as often as fucking possible. Finally she spoke. "If we are going to do this, there can't be anyone else."

My thoughts immediately went to Luke. I closed my eyes so she wouldn't see my anger. "I won't share you, Lexi."

She snorted, "I meant you, you male slut. No more groupies being sneaked onto the bus. No more whores lined up outside your dressing room."

"Of course not. Just you and me." She leaned into me, touching my lips with a feather light kiss. Then she ran her tongue along my lower lip. "Is that a 'yes Dash, I'd love to spend the next eight weeks underneath your hot body'?"

She shook her head as she giggled. "That was a yes, Dash, I'd love to make you my sex slave for the next eight weeks."

"I'll take it." I grabbed the back of her head and fused her mouth to mine. I needed to taste her. I needed to invade every inch of her. She moaned. I almost came in my pants. "Kitten, those sweet sounds you make are going to be the death of me." I felt her smile against my mouth. I rolled over on top of her, placing my dick right at her core, grinding against her slowly. She gasped. I groaned. "I want you so fucking much."

"I'm right here, Dash. Take me." She arched her neck, giving me better access.

I could feel her frantic pulse with my lips. "Believe me, baby, I will." I pulled her earlobe between my teeth and ran my hand down the side of her body, grazing her perfect breast. "But when I take you, an hour won't be nearly long enough. I want all night to touch you, to make you moan. And we'll be in Houston soon. So how about you let me spoon you while I take a nap?"

Chapter Ten

Lexi

I woke up to a banging on the door. "Lex! Dash! We're here. Get dressed." Smith could be an asshole. I rolled over to see Dash giving me a sleepy smile. "Time to go to work, rock star."

He lifted his wrist and checked the time. "Yes, sadly, it's time for me to go to work. The guys and I usually shower in our dressing room. There is just more space and more hot water. You and Amy get dressed here and then come meet us. I'll get one of the security guys to come and walk you over." He rolled out of bed and tripped over Dagger. Catching himself on the wall he cursed, "Damn. That dog takes up the whole room."

I reached over the side of the bed, petting Dagger. "Yeah, he isn't very compact. You should see his crate. It's massive. I don't even know if there will be room on the bus for it. I might have to leave him in the bathroom and hope for the best." The best being that he wouldn't eat the *whole* door trying to get out.

Dash leaned over Dags and stuck his tongue down my throat. I raised my eyebrows in question when he pulled back. "Just a little something for the road." He winked. "Bring Dags with you. We'll find him some doggie headphones so the show doesn't hurt his ears."

"Really? Are we allowed to do that?"

Dash threw his head back and laughed, "Kitten we are headlining a sold-out tour, there isn't much we aren't allowed to do."

"Spoiled little rock star." I rolled my eyes and threw the covers off. I was a little hot after that kiss.

Dash paused with his hand on the door and spun around slowly. "*Little* rock star? We both know that there is nothing little about me, Kitten." I threw a pillow at him as he walked out laughing. He was right though; I'd learned that this morning.

***

About an hour later, after both Amy and I had showered and gotten dressed, that guy Chase came and got us. Now we were all sitting in the guys' dressing room waiting for them to take the stage.

Dash had come through with some badass looking headphones for Dagger; they had a skull and cross bones on each side.

Dash and I were sitting on barstools—the band requested a bar in every dressing room apparently—with our legs intertwined. He was rubbing his hands up and down my leather leggings, coming very close to my ass every time. "Let's take a shot." He stood and went around the bar, reaching for a short green bottle.

"NO. No Jäger! Please don't even open the bottle. If I smell it, I'll puke. Anything but Jäger."

Dash slowly drew his hand away from the Jäger and reached for the Fireball. "Okkkkay, what's the deal with Jäger?" He got out 6 shot glasses and lined them up.

"Bad river trip in college, took one too many pulls off the Jäger bottle and threw up for hours. Pretty sure I had alcohol poisoning." I reached for one of the glasses. "Now whiskey, whiskey I can do just fine."

Dash came around the bar, put his hand on my hip and his mouth on mine before turning to the rest of the room. "Come on, let's take a shot. We need to celebrate." He waited until everyone had gathered around and had a glass in hand. "Here's to finally meeting Luke's two favorite girls. Here's to hiring a badass photographer, and here's to our new band mascot." He gestured to Dagger with his glass before slamming it back. Everyone else followed suit. The yellow light by the door turned green. Dash grabbed my hand and snapped his fingers at Dagger, pointing to his side. "Dags, come." My normally disobedient dog dutifully stood and walked over to us.

Luke threw his hands in the air. "This is bullshit." He got down eye level with Dagger. "I've known you since the day your mom brought you home. I've fed you, played with you, cleaned up your destructive messes…and you never listen to me. This guy?" He gestured to Dash with his thumb. "He's doing dirty things to your mom behind our backs. Yet you listen to him? I'm at a loss, Dagger, really I am."

I laughed and ruffled Luke's hair. "Don't take it personally, Lukey. He loves you." I waited until he stood and then made sure I looked him in the eye. "We both do." He gave me a nod and a small smile before pulling me in and kissing my forehead. Dash's hand tightened on mine, but he didn't say anything as we all walked out of the room. I knew Luke wasn't pumped about whatever was happening between Dash and I, but I needed Luke to know that no matter what, I loved him.

When we got to the stage Dash placed Dags earphones on his head. "Leave it, Dagger." Dagger huffed, but sat down. He put his finger under my chin and gave me a long lazy kiss. "Enjoy the show, spend some time with Amy, because as soon as I walk off the stage we're going to bed." I slapped his ass as he left.

The crowd went wild when the guys walked to their spots. Cameras were going off; people were screaming; a few girls were crying. I snapped a couple pictures of the tear-soaked girls. Amy came and stood next to me and leaned her head on my shoulder. "Can you believe that's Lukey out there? I still can't wrap my head around it."

I nodded. "I know. It's so surreal." Every part of the last two days was surreal. I was going on tour with a hella famous rock group. I was hired to take pictures for their next album. My pictures were going to be seen by millions of people. And the craziest part about it? I was semi-dating Dash Conner. "I'm going to miss you these next few weeks."

Amy laughed and gestured towards the stage. "Are you kidding me? Between partying with the rich and famous, working, and banging Dash…when exactly will you even have time to miss me?"

I stuck out my lower lip, making a sad face. "Times like right now. When I can feel the groupies shooting daggers at my back. When the boys are all busy working and I'm just standing off to the side with my camera and my dog." I reached down and patted Dags who was still wearing his headphones, just like Dash had told him to.

I looked back at the stage in time to see Dash wink at me. Not gonna lie, a hot guy winking at me in front of a thousand screaming fans, made me swoon a little. "So, I met this girl." He waited for the audience's cheers to die down. "She likes Van Morrison and I like her. So tonight we are going to do a little cover song if y'all don't mind." He smiled out at the crowd when they all applauded.

If I thought I was swooning before, it was nothing compared to how it felt hearing The Devil's Share doing a rocking cover of "He Ain't Give You None" for me. If I had any doubts about following through with our little arrangement, they flew out the window.

The rest of the show flew by, probably because I was starting to feel anxious about what was going to happen after. The whiskey and coke I'd been drinking was helping. Amy's flight left really early, so early that I would be telling her good-bye tonight. Luke and she had decided to get a hotel room close to the airport and spend all night watching movies and hanging out. I didn't know if that had been Amy's idea or Luke's. Either way, I wouldn't have to worry about pissing anyone off when I jumped into bed with Dash. I heard Smith yell, "Thank you, good night!" and my heart skipped a beat.

Chapter Eleven

Dash

The stage lights went down and I made a beeline for Lexi. No part of me was joking when I told her that I was walking off this stage and straight into her pants. I'd waited two days. I'd wooed her, spooned her, taken care of her dog and professed my "like" for her in front of a thousand people. That should prove to both her and Luke that I was into her.

When I got to her she was hugging Amy bye. "Ugh, I'm going to miss you."

"Me too, Lex. Have fun and take care of Lukey for me?"

I grabbed Lexi's hand. She hugged Amy one more time. "Of course I will. Have a safe flight."

I quickly hugged Amy and reminded Luke the bus pulled out at eight a.m. tomorrow. Amy's flight left at seven, so he should make it back in plenty of time. I pulled Lex to my side. I had Chase, my favorite security guy, walk in front of us to deflect the groupies. It was almost comical that his job with the groupies had changed overnight. Chase knew how to pick 'em. He could always tell the ones with fake IDs, and for some reason he was good at recognizing crazy when he saw it. "Did you like the show?"

She hugged me tighter. "Are you kidding me? I loved the show. Thanks for the song by the way." I took Dags leash from her hand. He seemed to pull her a little, but when I took him he fell into step. Maybe I *was* the dog whisperer. "So where next?"

"Starkville, Mississippi." I felt Lexi tense underneath me. "Playing at the stadium after a football game. It's more of a charity gig. Our manager went to Mississippi State. It's a really pretty drive from what I hear." She didn't say anything. "What? What's wrong?"

"Nothing. It is a pretty drive, I've actually made it before." She was biting her lip, trying not to react.

"If this has something to do with a piece of your missing virtue, I don't even want to know." That was the truth. I couldn't handle the thought of Lexi and another guy. It made want to punch someone. And I had never considered myself a jealous person. "Well?"

"What? You said you didn't want to know." She had let go of her lip and was full on smiling.

"You're right, I don't." I did. Sort of. It was one of those "you do but you don't" situations where what is in your head is hopefully worse than the reality. Luckily, we reached the bus and all conflicted thoughts left my mind as the majority of my blood headed south. I opened the door, ushering her and Dags inside. I locked the door behind me—all the guys had a key. When Lexi went to head to the kitchen I grabbed her hand and started to pull her down the hallway. "Nope. No detours."

She rolled her eyes. "I just wanted something to drink."

"There's whiskey in the bedroom." I led her to the room. Dagger followed and tried to get on the bed again. "Dags, no. Down." I pointed at the floor. He just stood there staring at me. "DOWN." Nothing. "Lexi what's wrong with your dog?"

"Maybe he knows what you're planning to do to me. Maybe he doesn't approve." She shrugged and leaned against the wall, her eyes dancing with humor.

I mumbled, "Maybe Luke put him up to it." She laughed but I wasn't joking. I heard the door to the bus open and voices in the living room. I opened the door and stuck my head out. "Smith. Smith! Come here."

He came down the hall looking bored, followed by Jacks who wore a shit-eating grin. "Need me to show you how it's done?"

I flipped him off. "Are y'all going out tonight?"

Smith shook his head. "Nah. My dick is still recovering from the head from hell."

I winced. "Jesus. Was it that bad?"

"I told you it was! *Now* can Lex rub my hair and feel sorry for me?"

I heard Lexi giggle behind me. She found all this very amusing. "No, she's busy. I need you to take Dagger. He won't lie down and he keeps looking at me. I think he's judging me."

Jacks chuckled, "Come here Dagger, you're throwing your new daddy off his game." I flipped him off again, opening the door so Dags could clomp his way down the hall with Jacks and Smith.

I shut and locked the door, then turned to find Lexi lying on the bed in nothing but some black lacey panties and a bra that barely contained her breasts. "I guess the wooing is over then?"

She laughed. "Wooing is over. You did a really great job though. I was actually impressed."

I peeled off my shirt and stepped out of my jeans and boxers. I wasn't shy, no reason to be; I was blessed. "You ain't seen nothing yet, Kitten."

Chapter Twelve

Lexi

Holy mother of… He was so gorgeous he looked fake. Tattoos crept up and down his lean muscular arms. Music notes littered his toned stomach. His dark hair was a mess from performing all night. I stared at him openly, smiling. "Well? You gonna make a move or what?"

He placed his knee on the bed, crawling up body. "Just waiting for you to get done eye fucking me." I laughed. He wasn't wrong. He put his hands on my knees, spreading them to make room for himself between my legs. He put his cock at my core and moved just enough to cause some friction. He kissed my chest, moving the straps of my bra out of the way, kissing my shoulders. When his mouth finally found mine I couldn't contain my moan. Everything he did was so perfect; he knew just the right way to push every button, to make me want to beg for it. "Dash. Please." My words came out as a whisper. I couldn't seem to find my voice.

He reached into the nightstand. My eyes followed his movements. The top drawer was full of condoms—like filled to the brim. There had to be a hundred of them. I inwardly rolled my eyes. *Fucking rock stars.* No pun intended. Dash put the condom under the pillow and continued to torture me. He nibbled and licked his way around my body. Taking his time he used his fingers to bring me to the brink time and again, only to pull back. I ran my nails up and down his back, scratching him lightly. I wanted to leave my mark. The feel of his body against mine was pure perfection. He kissed me like his life depended on it. I felt like I was being worshipped.

Finally he grabbed the condom, rolled it on and positioned his long length at my core. "Look at me, Kitten." I did as I was told. "Tell me you want this as much as I do. I need to here you say the words. Say that you are right here with me, no doubts."

I placed my hands at his hips, pulling him forward, easing him inside of me. "I want you, I want this." Once he was buried to the hilt we both let out a breath I didn't know we'd been holding. He filled me completely. He filled me in the most amazing way possible. When he started to move, my body started to shiver. He was that good. Every thrust was perfect. His body was made for mine. "Oh God, Dash. Don't fucking stop."

He chuckled, "You have a mouth on you, Kitten." He slammed into me twice before nuzzling my ear. "Say it again."

I brought my legs up higher on his waist, wanting him deeper, harder. "Don't stop fucking me. Oh God, don't stop." And he didn't. It felt like he was inside me for hours. Every time my cries would build, he'd pull back so I didn't finish. He was prolonging this, taking his time. It was becoming too much, too intense. My need to fly over the edge was bordering on painful. I scratched my nails down his back and bit his chest. "Please. I need…"

I felt his body tighten, the sounds that were coming out of his throat were purely animalistic. My body responded instantly. I couldn't stop my orgasm this time even if I had wanted too. It overwhelmed me in the most amazing way possible. I'd never had an orgasm like the one Dash had just given me.

He gripped my hips harder, driving into me over and over again. "Oh God…"

When he came the sensation of him pulsing inside of me was so hard it sent me flying over the edge again. "Oh God!"

"Oh God, Lexi." His head was resting on my shoulder. We were both still panting, trying to catch our breath. I trailed my hands up and down his back. He was covered in a fine sheen of sweat—hell, we both were.

"Dash, that was so fucking amazing and—"

"Oh God." I felt Dash pull out.

I giggled, "Are you still coming? Damn, you're right, new level of impressed here."

Dash sat back on the bed, his head in his hands. "Oh God. Lex, are you on the pill?"

I felt the blood drain from my face. "No. What? Why? What happened?"

"The condom broke…well it fucking exploded." I followed his gaze down to his hands. No joke, the condom was shredded. "Who the hell isn't on the pill these days?!"

"Excuse me? Who the fuck doesn't pull out?! I should be the one freaking out here. How many girls have you banged in the last thirty days?! Holy shit." I was suddenly sweating for a completely different reason. I piled my hair on top of my head and shook out my hands. They felt like they were going numb. "Okay, okay, just give me second to think."

"I'm sorry I shouldn't have yelled at you. You're right. I should have pulled out." He mumbled under his breath, "I always fucking pull out." He shrugged. "And I've never not worn a condom and this is the first one to ever break. I swear, I'm clean."

I shook my head, holding up my hand to silence him. "Stop talking. Let me count."

Dash had gotten up and thrown the condom away. He was digging around in the drawer checking expiration dates before tossing the condoms to the side. "Count? Count what?"

"Stop talking." Maybe we had nothing to worry about, maybe it was the wrong time of the month and everything would be just fine. After all there were only like five days out of the month that you could actually get pregnant. I closed my eyes and started counting back to my last period. Nope. Not fine, not even in the realm of fine. "Okay, I don't want to alarm you, but this bad."

"How bad?" He stood up and started pacing the small room, buck naked. Good thing he had sent Dagger out; he wouldn't have had any room otherwise.

"Let's just say, if we were trying to make a baby…now would be the perfect time to give it a shot." I watched as Dash crumpled to the floor. It wasn't a funny situation, but it was too comical not to laugh as he crawled to a nearby shelf and grabbed a bottle of whiskey. He crawled to the bed and came to sit next to me. "What now?"

He opened the bottle, took a pull and handed it to me. "Now we get drunk. Then we screw some more, because what could it hurt at this point…and in the morning we wake up early and go get that morning after pill thing. Problem solved, easy peasy."

Was that what I wanted? Was I okay with that? My mind was a jumble of thoughts and what ifs. I wasn't ready to be a parent. Dash and I weren't even dating. I took a big gulp off the bottle. The warm liquid traveled down my throat and I could literally feel my anxiety dissipating. "You're calmer than I thought you'd be." I took another drink. "It's that simple? We keep fucking and drinking and then stumble to the nearest drug store thoroughly satisfied and completely hung over? Seems kind of irresponsible."

Dash took the bottle back, drank some, and then kissed my shoulder. "Sounds fun though." He placed a soft kiss on my neck, then another under my ear. "Plus, I'm still horny. Once wasn't enough. I need more." He ran his finger from my neck to my nipple. "I promise I'll be more careful this time. Trust me?"

My eyes closed in ecstasy; just his touch could bring me to my knees. I should tell him no. I should put my clothes back on and take this as a sign. But I wanted him too. I needed to have him inside again. I knew I wouldn't be able to walk away from him. Why fight it? "Yes."

"Good girl, Kitten." Those were the last words I remembered hearing that night.

Chapter Thirteen

Dash

I woke up for the second morning in a row completely tangled up in
Lexi. Her eyes were closed, her breathing steady. Our room smelled
like sex and whiskey. We had spent the remainder of the night
drinking and fucking. Nonstop. We laughed and danced and kissed.
It was the best night I'd ever spent with a girl, aside from the
shredded condom incident. But I was going to fix that ASAP, no
worries. I sat up and let my eyes rake down her body. She was so
damn beautiful. Her hair shone in the sunlight. Sunlight? Why was
there sunlight? We had set an alarm to get up at seven and go to the
drug store. I checked my watch. *One p.m.?! Holy fucking shit.*
"Kitten, wake up. Lexi! Get up, baby." I jumped out of bed and
threw on my jeans from last night. Lexi threw a pillow at my head. I
slapped her sexy naked ass. "Lexi, wake the hell up. We overslept by
like five fucking hours."

At that she jolted up right. Her hair was all over the place and I
was pretty sure she had a hickey on her neck. Oops. "I thought you
set an alarm?!" She was pulling on clothes from the floor. The shirt
she threw on belonged to Jacks, but at least the pants were hers.

"I did. I don't know what happened! Maybe it was all the
whiskey or the constant orgasms. This is partly your fault, you
know." I stepped over countless condom wrappers and threw open
the bedroom door. I raced down the hall with Lex right behind me.
"Stop the bus! For the love of God please stop the bus." The entire
band was sitting in the living room, staring at us like we had lost our
damn minds.

Smith raised his eyebrows in question. "Uh…first of all, your
pants are on backwards. Second of all, why?"

Lexi and I looked at each other. I took a deep breath. "I need to
go to the store. The drug store."

Jacks held up his hand for a high five. "You two went through
all those fucking condoms?! Holy shit! You *are* a rock sex god." We
all ignored him. "Is Lexi wearing my shirt?"

Luke gestured out the window. "Look even if we did stop the bus we haven't passed another car in an hour, let alone any drug stores."

Smith shrugged. "What? Are you a condom snob now? Just wait till we get to the next gas station."

Lexi sat on the floor next to Dagger, leaning her face into his neck. I had to make this right. I had to be the man and find a way to fix this. I walked back into the bedroom and pulled out my cell phone and called Chase. He was following the bus in a U-Haul. "Hey man, I need you to do me a huge fucking favor. I'll pay you time and a half and I'll owe you one."

"Sure, bud, what's up?"

I took a deep breath. I trusted Chase, but still if it got out into the media that Dash Conner had an employee out trying to score him the morning after pill…it could have some drastic repercussions, especially in this part of the country. "I need you to hop on my bike and find me a drug store. I need the morning after pill. And I need it like yesterday." There was a few seconds of silence on the other end of the line. "Chase?"

"Yeah I'm here, just you know, in a car full of people. So…I'll get it done. No worries."

"Thanks, man." I hung up and went back into the living room. No one was talking. Luke looked pissed, Jacks looked excited, and Smith looked confused. Lexi? Lexi was harder to read. She was still sitting by Dagger, but she was looking at Luke. I sat down next to her and cupped her face in my hands, kissing her sweetly before whispering, "I've got it covered, okay?" I rested my forehead against hers and I felt her nod. Suddenly this image of Lexi with a round belly popped into my head. It made me smile. Whoa, was that what I wanted? Did I—

Luke cleared this throat, "What the fuck is going on?"

I leaned back on Dagger's side and closed my eyes. "Nothing, man. Leave it alone."

Luke stood and called Dagger to his side of the room, making me fall back on to the floor. "Like hell I'll leave it alone. Did you hurt her? I'll kill you."

I stood up, taking a step towards him. "Mind your own business. This is between me and Lex." Luke took a step towards me. We were getting closer to throwing punches with every word.

Lexi stood up between us, putting a hand on each of our chests. I hated that she was touching him. She was mine. "Both of you, stop. You are acting ridiculous." She looked up at Luke. "Of course he didn't hurt me. What kind of question is that?" I put my hand over hers and took a step back, bringing her with me. Luke narrowed his eyes but kept his mouth shut. Lexi shrugged. "It's not that big of deal, really. A condom broke."

Both Jacks and Smith jumped to their feet. Jacks ran to the bedroom calling over his shoulder, "Did you check the dates?! Are they faulty?"

Smith started pacing the room. "Was it just that one? Did you test others? We should throw them all out and get new ones." Jacks came into the room holding handfuls of empty condom wrappers. "Good, looks like they tested a bunch of them."

Chapter Fourteen

Lexi

Oddly, Jacks had broken some of the tension in the room when he walked out carrying all of our condom wrappers. Now everyone knew without a doubt that I had slept with Dash. Everything was out in the open. But I could feel the tension rolling off of Luke. I couldn't just sit here in a room full of loaded silence. "Who's hungry? It's lunchtime right?"

Smith had sat back down in the recliner. He was using his foot to rub Dagger's belly. "Dags told me that he wanted you to make chicken salad for lunch."

"*Dags* isn't allowed to eat chicken salad. He's mayonnaise intolerant. Believe me, we learned that the hard way." I ruffled Smith's hair.

He looked up at me. "Dags said that since you kept me up all night, you should make *me* chicken salad."

"I am almost positive I was not the reason you were up last night. Didn't you have a room full of groupies to work through?"

"Not last night, I was still in recovery. And you totes kept me up, you're a screamer Lex." Smith pointed at Jacks. "Dude, back me up."

Dash reached over and punched Smith in the arm. "That's enough." His words sounded harsh, but the smile on his face gave him away.

"You two bang until five a.m. and I'm the one getting hit? I went the longest walk I could." Smith rubbed his arm, bottom lip sticking out like a toddler.

Jacks was back to lying on the floor next to Dagger. "You should have worn earplugs like I did. Between those and the sound of the Dagmeister snoring, I slept like a baby. Can I have a sandwich too?"

I glanced over at Dash. He was staring at me wearing a horny smile. "I think after lunch we need to take a nap, Kitten."

I bit my lip and shook my head. Of course knowing that everyone heard me scream his name would turn him on. His ego was the size of Texas. I rolled my eyes and headed towards the kitchen. "Anyone else want one? Luke? Dash, are you hungry?"

Dash chuckled, "I'm suddenly starving, baby."

Luke threw down his phone and stomped past me. "I'll help you, Lex." We all heard him start slamming cabinets.

Dash went to stand but I put my hand on his shoulder to stop him. "It's fine, Dash. I can handle Luke." He took my hand in his and kissed my palm.

"I know you can handle him, Lex. But there is no reason for him to take out his shit on you. If he's pissed at me, he should take it out on me. If he doesn't want to see or hear about us being together, he needs to ride with the road crew." He looked towards the kitchen. "I mean it, Lex. If I hear him raise his voice one time, I'm coming in there."

I popped Smith on the back of the head as I walked by. "Do you have to be such a damn instigator?" When I got in the kitchen Luke had all the ingredients on the counter and was opening a can of chicken. "Luke, I—"

He whirled on me. "Are you kidding me, Lex? I mean I knew he wanted you, but really? You are way too good for him. You deserve better and you fucking know it. Stop selling yourself short. I thought you were over the bad boy stage." Thank hell he was whisper-yelling and not yelling-yelling.

"Luke, that's enough. I am an adult, I make my own choices, and right now I am *choosing* to spend time getting to know Dash and—"

"Getting to know? Or fucking?" I could tell he regretted the words the instant they left his mouth; his face said it all.

"I'm going to give you a free pass on that one because I know you are just looking out for me. But you don't need to protect me from Dash. He has been nothing but amazing to me. He is sweet and romantic and caring." I stood next to him at the counter and went about making lunch for everyone. "Now stop worrying so damn much and have fun with me. I mean, come on! Once in a lifetime stuff happening right now."

He didn't smile like I thought he would, instead he looked sad as he said, "Twice in a lifetime, Lex. It may have been a way less glamorous tour, but we've done this together before." He looked down and sighed, "Let's just hope that this tour ends differently than the last." Then he left.

***

I was lying on the couch with my legs across Dash's lap. He was absentmindedly rubbing my calves. I had my camera out and I snapped a few pics of Dash's hands on my legs. Luke was playing Xbox with Jacks on the floor, leaning against the couch near my head. Every once in a while I'd reach over and scratch his scalp. Every time I did it though, Dash would shoot me a look. Not an angry look, more annoyed, I guess. Luke's words had me distracted all through lunch. I didn't want to ruin this tour for him by sleeping with Dash…but why the hell would me sleeping with Dash ruin the tour? Yes, Luke had always been protective, but he'd never tried to tell me whom I could or couldn't date. Not that Dash and I were dating…

"Dash and Lexi are dating."

I laughed nervously, "Uh, Smith, I don't know if—"

Smith held up his iPad. There was a picture of me standing side stage at the last show and Dash looking over at me. "It's on this gossip website I follow. 'Sorry to be the bearer of bad news, but Dash Conner is off the market, ladies. He has been seen two nights in a row making eyes at one Alexis Grant. The two met through Luke Matthews, The Devil's Share's newest member. It's rumored that Alexis has even joined Dash on tour.'"

My whole body tensed up. How would Dash react to that? How would Luke?

"Don't tell people you follow a gossip website, dude. It makes you sound like a dumb ass." Jacks pointed his controller at the TV, furiously hitting the same button again and again. "Dammit! Luke killed me."

Smith chuckled, "Luke's gonna kill Dash next, now that he is officially dating Lexi."

"For the love of everything holy, Smith, shut up!" I hadn't meant to shout that, it just came out. I looked down the couch to find Dash smiling back at me. Holy hell he was handsome—even in jeans and a plain white t-shirt, hair all a mess from me pulling on it last night. Oh wow, now I was having flashbacks to last night—the sight of that sexy head of hair between my thighs. Dash winked at me. Could he tell what I was thinking?

Luke shrugged. "Why would I be mad because some gossip magazine is spouting bull? Not the first time and I'm sure it won't be the last." Luke glanced at me before looking back to his game.

Dash sat forward, his elbows on his knees. He was kind of crushing my legs, but the serious look on his face kept me from saying anything. "What is that supposed to mean exactly? Why is it such 'bull' to think of me and Lex dating?"

Luke chuckled, "Come on, you can't be serious?"

Dash stared at him, face set in hard lines.

Luke sighed and shook his head. "I've watched you jump from chick to chick for the last six months. You don't date, Dash. You play and you use and you move on."

I thought Dash was going to explode, we all did. Smith, Jacks, and I held our breath waiting for his reaction. We were all shocked when he calmly turned to me and said, "Kitten, do you in anyway feel like I am using you or stringing you along?"

I shook my head. "No."

He nodded. "Okay good." Dash stood and pulled me to my feet. "I am only going to say this one more fucking time so I need all of you to listen real close. I like Lexi. I want Lexi. I want her here with me all the time. I am not using her. I am not playing with her. If anyone questions that again, I'm going to start throwing punches. Understood?"

Jacks grinned. "Yes, daddy, we all understand how much you like mommy."

Luke said nothing. He didn't even look in our direction. Smith chuckled and closed the iPad.

Dash cracked his knuckles. "Good. Now we're going to go take a nap." He picked me up and slung me over his shoulder. "And by 'take a nap,' I mean get naked and fool around." When we got to the bedroom Dash dumped me on the bed before turning to shut and lock the door. He pointed at me. "You, take off Jacks's shirt. Seeing you wear another guy's shirt has irritated me all afternoon. Didn't I tell you the other day not to do that?"

I looked down smiling. "I'm so sorry. Next time we sleep through the alarm we set so we could go buy the morning after pill, I'll try and throw on my clothes instead of Jacks's." I tossed the shirt at Dash. He dropped it onto the floor and jumped on the bed. We lay on our sides, facing each other, bodies pressed together. "Are you freaking out? About the condom thing?"

He trailed his hand down the side of my body, gripping my hip and pulling my pelvis more firmly against his. "Not really. Are you?"

I shrugged. "I don't know. With everything going on with Luke today, I haven't really had all that much time to think about it."

"Well, Chase is getting us what we need. But as far as Luke goes…I don't really know what to tell you, Lex. You've known him longer than I have."

Dash cupped my breast in his hand, kneading it and making it hard for me to form coherent thoughts. "That's the problem though, isn't it? I've known him longer. He thinks he can boss me around and tell me what to do and who to do it with."

"Lex, are you sure there isn't more going on between you and Luke? If there is something you need to tell me… There has to be more to y'all's history."

Was there? Did that one memory between Luke and I, all those years ago, really matter? Maybe I was delusional in thinking it didn't. It was really Luke's story to tell, but this was my budding relationship with Dash on the line so I took a deep breath. "About five years ago, I went on this small tour with Luke and his band. It was the summer after my junior year and Luke asked me to come. They wanted some pictures of them playing, but mainly it was just an excuse to party. They played smaller venues, bars mostly, but they had a really strong following. The band…those guys all grew up together. They were as much his family as me or Amy. Everything started out fine. They would play; then we would drink and party. But things went south towards the end. The band was more interested in the drugs than the music. They needed coke to get them up and playing and then sleeping pills and tequila to get them to crash at night." The next part was harder for me to talk about. Maybe that's why Luke never told anyone the story; it was just too hard. I cleared my throat. "The bands lead singer, Sam, he um…one night he didn't come down so well. He kind of lost it. He got really angry and went into this crazy rage fit. We were all staying in this hotel suit together. I was the only one home. The rest of the band was still out at the bar. When I tried to calm him down, he grabbed me and threw me against the wall. He was so strong, so strung out. I mean his eyes…I didn't even recognize him, you know?" I felt Dash's body go ridged against mine. I closed my eyes, trying to even my breathing, there was no going back now. "Anyway, Luke came in and found him standing over me. Luke beat the shit out of him. The other guys had to pull him off of Sam. He would have killed him." And I would have let him. The one thing neither one of us has ever told anyone, not another living soul, was that Sam had his pants unbuttoned and had just ripped off my shirt. I was kind of floating in and out of consciousness at that point, but I would never forget the sound of his zipper.

I watched Dash's throat work to swallow. "He attacked you?"

"My head hit the wall pretty hard, and he slapped me around a little bit. Luke took me to the hospital. I was fine. Luke wasn't though. He blamed himself. He said he should have never left me alone. And for the rest of the tour, he didn't. Luke barely let me out of his sight. He stopped partying with band, stopped all the drugs. He told me that I saved his life, but the truth was, he saved mine."

"Luke kept touring? Even with you being attacked?"

I placed my hand over Dash's heart. "Luke wanted to leave the tour, but I wouldn't let him. I didn't want one stupid mistake to ruin everything for them. Sam didn't remember anything the next morning. I was a little bruised, a little shaken up but totally fine. I didn't think it was worth ruining their futures. In the end though…it didn't matter. Everyone except for Luke kept doing coke, which turned into heroin, which turned into meth. The band broke up six months later."

Dash ran his thumb along my lower lip. "You are a remarkable person, Lexi. Your heart is so good, so strong. I can see now, I can see why Luke acts the way he does. Why he's in love with you."

I shook my head, "Luke isn't in love with me, Dash. He thinks I saved his life. He thinks without me he would have nothing, be nothing. He blames himself for what happened with Sam. In his mind, I'm his, to keep safe and to protect." I shrugged. "He's just having a hard time letting go."

Dash leaned in and pressed his lips lightly to mine. "Well, I'll just have to convince him that while you are here, on this tour, you are mine…to keep safe and protect."

I giggled, "The broken condom probably didn't do anything to help your case." He kissed me again, harder this time. My whole body responded to his kisses. My heart raced, my core clenched, my nipples peaked. I had never felt like this before, never felt this type of desire. I loved it. I wanted more. "Dash."

"Lexi." I could feel him smile against my neck.

"I want you."

He chuckled close to my ear, "Of course you do, Kitten."

I reached between our bodies and stuck my hand down his pants grabbing his cock. I slowly began to stroke twisting up and down. He groaned and nibbled his way down my neck. I smiled. "I want you to fuck me."

Dash pulled his mouth from my breast and looked at me, grinning from ear to ear. "Yes, ma'am."

Chapter Fifteen

Dash

I couldn't sleep. My mind wouldn't let me. The things Lex had told me about her and Luke, it brought everything into perspective. Everything made sense now. Of course he was trying to save her from me; he would always try to save her from the things that could hurt her. My track record wasn't so great, as he liked to point out in front of her as often as he could. And Luke had no way to know that I would rather die than make her feel one ounce of pain. How could I express it to him when I barely understood it myself? Lexi had told me her truth. She was so open so trusting with herself. She made me want to give her everything, tell her everything. I ended up unloading all my stress on her. About life, about the past, about the future. Smith was becoming such a damn pain in the ass. The drummer that Luke replaced was his cousin. Smith and Jared had both gotten deep into speed. Smith had cleaned up and Jared hadn't. We couldn't have an unreliable band member. We were too big for that. Everyone would notice. But since he and Jared had been so close, Smith was acting out—as passive aggressively as he possibly could. I knew Jared still talked to Smith, still called to give him shit and ask him if he needed any speed. Jared was bad for Smith, and if I didn't watch him closely, Jared would pull him back under. Their family history was so fucked up it wouldn't take much. I couldn't get Jacks to take life seriously for more than five minutes at a time. I was almost positive that he had a gaming problem. I was constantly having to watch him and keep him out of trouble. Well, me and Luke. No wonder Luke was so good at watching Smith and Jacks; he didn't want history to repeat itself. And the cherry on top? The one fucking time in my life that I hadn't pulled out, the condom exploded. I looked down at Lexi. She had fallen asleep on my chest, and I adored it. I was turning into a sappy romantic bastard, but oddly enough, I didn't mind. My phone vibrated on the nightstand. Chase was calling. "Hello?"

"Hey, Dash, it's Chase."

"Yeah, what's up? Please tell me you got what I needed."

"Uh…actually man, it's proving a little difficult to find the morning after pill in Mississippi."

"What? Why? Isn't it like a nationwide thing?"

"I thought it was, but it turns out that if a pharmacy is locally owned, which most of these are…then they don't *have* to carry it."

"Okay. Okay. Wow. I am really trying not to freak out here, man."

"There is one more pharmacy that I'm going to try. It's about an hour outside of Starkville. It's on my way to you guys. I'll see you soon."

"Thanks, Chase. Be safe." I hung up and then proceeded to squeeze my phone so hard I was surprised it didn't crack. Then, to continue my silent fit, I punched the air a few times. Once my little tantrum was over, I realized I wasn't even all that upset. This must be how a two-year-old feels. React first, think later. A two-year-old, or a twenty-seven year-old Jacks.

"I can feel you freaking out. What's wrong?" Lex mumbled against my chest without opening her eyes. "Was that Chase?"

I took a deep breath. "Yeah, it seems that he is having a hard time trying to procure our little pill here in the Deep South."

Lexi smiled against my chest. "Why don't you just let me take a car and drive back to Texas? I can get it back in Houston."

I shook my head. "Absolutely not, Kitten. Our relationship is all over the Internet. People would recognize you. Either they would think you and I needed the pill—and again the 'Deep South' would judge me and the band—or they would think you were having some kind of affair or something. They would blow this up and it would end up being a big to-do. Plus, there is no way Luke, let alone I, would let you make that drive alone. So we'd end up having to cancel the show."

"I could call my doctor's office and see if they could call in a prescription."

I shrugged. "Same deal there. People would recognize your name. It'd be all over the news. We have like, what, sixty more hours? Let's just see if Chase can get this done."

"Doctors can't share patient information like that. It's against the law."

I chuckled. "Doctors can't, but that doesn't stop their employees from talking. Ask Jacks about The Clap Incident of 2012."

Lexi wrinkled her cute little nose. "The Clap, like the band?"
I shook my head, "Nope."

Chapter Sixteen

Lexi

Dagger and I were sitting in the band's dressing room. I was under strict instructions to wait here for Chase. Dash had tried to call him a few times before he went on but he couldn't get a hold of him. I was using the time to take some pictures—the line of shot glasses on the bar, Jacks' vintage Aerosmith t-shirt draped over a chair, Smith's chewed on pencil lying in his guitar case. All these little things made up this band, gave insight into who they were and how they lived. I loved how the right picture could make something as simple as a spilled bottle of Jack Daniels look like art.

The concert was playing over a speaker in the room. I smiled when I heard Dash address the stadium. "So I heard a rumor today that I have a girlfriend." There was a pause. I could imagine him winking at the crowd. "It's true." I collapsed into the nearest chair. Dash just called me his girlfriend. He just announced to the world we were dating. Holy freaking hell. I pulled out my phone and called Amy.

"Did you know your picture is all over the Internet?"

"Hello to you too, Ams."

"Sorry, hi. Did you know your picture is all over the Internet?"

"Yes, Smith brought that to our attention earlier today. Caused a little argument between Dash and Luke."

"I take it Lukey doesn't approve of you and Dash?"

"His irritation with the situation ebbs and flows…. Dash actually just announced to the stadium that the rumors were true and he did have a girlfriend."

"He means you?"

"Well I would hope to God he means me. I'm the one sleeping with him."

"Mmmmm…how was it? I need details."

"It was mind blowing. We literally had sex for hours last night, and twice again this afternoon. He is every fantasy I've ever had."

"I imagine. And when I say I imagine, I mean I'm literally sitting here with my eyes closed, imagining it."

"You are such a spaz." I wanted to tell Amy about the broken condom and the yet-to-show-up morning after pill. But I couldn't do it. I was starting to get nervous about it and telling Amy would make it all too real. "I miss you Amy, so freaking much."

"I miss you too, Lex. Have fun with your new rock star boyfriend."

"Oh I will."

"I hate you."

"I love you, Amy."

"Love you more."

Just as I was hanging up the phone the door to the dressing opened and Chase walked in. His hands were empty. But before I could calmly and rationally ask him if my pill was in his pocket, the band filed in. Luke headed to the bar and poured himself a shot; no doubt Dash's little confession had set him off. Smith grabbed his jacket and headed next door to a room I was almost positive was filled with willing and able girls. Jacks came in and grabbed Dagger's face, "I will see you later tonight my little cuddle buddy," before grabbing his stuff and following Smith out the door.

Dash was the last one in the room. "Hey, Kitten." He put his arms around my waist lifting me up for a kiss. "Did Chase come by?"

I pulled back and pointed to the corner were Chase was standing, still empty handed. "You walked right past him."

Dash turned, smiling. "Hey man, sorry, I didn't see you there. Did you get our stuff?"

"Don't freak out but I couldn't get it." Chase held out his hands, like he was trying to warn off a wild animal. "The last place I checked had it, but would have required Lexi's ID to purchase it."

I watched Dash's smile fall slightly. "Okay…and why are we not supposed to freak out?"

"I called my sister that lives in Dallas. She's going to go pick one up and overnight it to the hotel where we're staying in Tennessee. It should be there waiting for y'all tomorrow afternoon."

Dash walked over to Chase and pulled him in for a hug. "You are a fucking genius!" He pointed to both Luke and me. "Let's take a shot."

Luke poured himself another. "Way ahead of ya."

Dash pushed Chase towards the bar. "You have the rest of the night off, have a few drinks with us." He came over and wrapped his arms around me whispering, "Just a few shots and we'll sneak out. All I could think about while I was out there singing was how badly I wanted to get back inside you."

"Hey, Lex, they have a kegorater in here. You up for some power pitcher?" Luke held up a plastic pitcher with a smile on his face.

I laughed, "Have I ever turned down power pitcher? Ever? No, sir. Let's play." Luke had probably guessed at what Dash whispered in my ear; the way he was plastered against my ass wasn't subtle. But Luke just looked so damn happy about playing that I couldn't turn him down.

"What's power pitcher? Is that like power hour?" Chase took the shot of whiskey Luke had left out for him.

"It's like power hour for tiny little college co-eds who don't have the stomach capacity for power hour." Luke winked at me.

I pointed at him. "Or underage drummers who don't have the tolerance."

He laughed. "Touché. It's a game we used to play—you fill up a pitcher full of beer, line up shot glasses and take shots until the beer is gone."

Dash mumbled under his breath, "At least it's a fast game."

I stood on tiptoe to whisper in his ear, "If you play nice with Luke right now, I'll play *very* nice with you later." Two could play the dirty whispered words game.

Dash smiled at Luke. "All right man, line 'em up. This sounds like fun."

Chapter Seventeen

Dash

There were four of us, so we had to play four fucking rounds of that stupid game before Lexi and I could leave. I had Dags leash in one hand, Lexi's hand in the other, and we were on our way back to the bus. Back to our bedroom…back to our bed. I was pretty damn happy.

"Dash! Dash! Is that Alexis? Is that your girlfriend? Is that your dog? Did y'all buy it together?"

There were reporters waiting for us outside the stadium. What the hell were reporters doing in fucking Starkville, Mississippi? There was nothing here except for the university and some stupid camo company. "Just keep your head down, Kitten. Keep walking." I shouldn't have given Chase the rest of the night off. I made a mental note to always have security with us from now on when we were walking to and from the venues. I didn't want Lexi getting ambushed when she was alone. Eventually we got close enough to the bus that the road crew heard all the commotion and came out to help us inside. "Hey, are you okay?"

"I'm fine, really, no worries."

"I'm gonna text the guys, let them know what to expect when they walk out the door." I pulled out my phone and texted my band mates while I used my body to herd Lex towards the bedroom.

"Impatient much?"

I locked the door behind me. "Hey, I played nice, just like you asked." I snapped and pointed to the ground. "Dagger, lay down." He blinked at me, still as a statue. I got down eye level with him. "Dagger, you listen to me all day, except when it's bedtime. I know what you're up to, and it isn't going to work. Now lie down, or you'll have to sleep in the living room alone." I stood and pointed to the floor. He huffed and snorted, but eventually lay down. I sat on the bed and reached for Lexi's hand, pulling her between my legs. "I want to talk to you about something."

She climbed onto my lap and placed her hands on my shoulders. "So talk."

I was suddenly nervous to ask her. Why was I being such a pussy? It's not like I was asking the girl to marry me. Or to do anal. "I haven't been in a monogamous relationship since I was seventeen years-old and—"

"You haven't had a girlfriend in over twelve years?! Good God, I seriously don't even want to guess at how many women you've slept with."

She visibly shivered. Great, maybe not the best opener for what I wanted to ask her. "Yeah, I'm a whore. I'm a very careful whore though. I've never had sex without a condom before, and I was thinking since you'll be taking the pill tomorrow anyway…maybe tonight, we could just not use one?" I lifted her shirt above her head. "It's actually all I've been thinking about since I got on stage tonight." I kissed her chest. "I almost forgot the words to a song that I have been playing live for five years." I placed my hands on her waist picking her up and spinning us both onto the bed. "But if you aren't into it, then that's okay." I pulled her jeans off and tossed them onto the floor. "What do you think?" I quickly removed all my clothes and lay back down beside her, brushing a strand of hair off her shoulder.

"On one hand, that sounds highly irresponsible and foolish."

"And on the other?" I held my breath.

Lexi let out a long sigh. "On the other? That sounds like it would feel reallllly good." She placed her leg over my hip, aligning our bodies.

"Really?" I was so happy I wanted to cry. "Oh wow, it's insane how excited I am right now. I feel like I'm about to lose my virginity all over again." She giggled and I captured the sweet sounds in my mouth. I let my hands roam all over her tight little body. I wanted her to want me so bad that she couldn't think straight. I grabbed her hands and threaded our fingers together. I brought our hands over her head and held her in place while I positioned myself at her core. Inch by slow tantalizing inch I entered Lexi. Being inside her bare was the most amazing feeling. It was like the best sex I've ever had, times one thousand. I wasn't going to last too long, not this first time. "Lexi, baby, you feel so fucking good." I rolled us over so that she was on top of me. I needed her to take charge, take what she needed, and fast. I used one hand to guide her hip, setting a nice rhythm. I trailed my other hand up her body, between her breasts and rested it at the base of her throat.

She moaned and leaned into my hand, "Dash…oh my God."

I closed my eyes; the sight of her riding me was too much. "Come for me, Kitten."

She moaned and pressed her throat against my hand a little harder before shattering around me. I rolled her back over, slammed into her a few more times and then pulled out and shot my come all over her beautiful stomach.

***

I woke up the next morning to complete silence, well, other than the sound of Lex breathing beside me and Dags snoring on the floor. Last night had been the best night of my life, hands down. Lexi was going to have to get on birth control ASAP, as I never wanted to have sex with a condom again. Wait. Why was it so quiet? Even if everyone was still asleep, there should be road noise. We were supposed to leave Mississippi at eight a.m. to head to Tennessee. I checked my watch. Yeah it was eleven already. We couldn't already be there could we? I got up and pulled on a pair of jeans. When I opened the bedroom door Dagger got up; the jingle from his collar woke Lex.

"Hey, where are you going?"

I leaned down and kissed her bare shoulder. Lexi just slept naked now. She realized quickly there was no use in putting clothes on, because I'd just take them off at some point in the night. "I think we might have stopped for gas. I'm going to take Dags for a walk real quick."

She yawned and lay back against the pillows. "Okay, thanks. I took him out around five this morning but I'm sure he would love another walk."

"You took Dagger for a walk at five o'clock this morning? Alone?! Tell me you didn't."

Lex raised her eyebrows and pursed her sexy lips. "Uh…I didn't?"

I shook my head. "Please don't do that again. Wake me up and I'll take him. It's not safe, Lex."

"Dags is my responsibility—"

I cut her off. "And you are mine. So just wake me up, okay?"

"Okay." She stretched her arms over her head. The sheet slipped down her body, exposing her breasts. She made no move to cover up. I loved how comfortable she was around me. She looked edible. Lexi laughed, "Don't even think about it Dash. I need a break. I think you broke me."

I wore a very smug male smile all the way down the hall, and out the door. Then, when I realized that the bus had not fucking moved since last night and we weren't almost to Tennessee, my smile fell. Chase was talking to our driver. Jacks was sitting on the grass with his head in his hands and Luke's fingers were flying over the keyboard on his phone. "What the hell is going on? Why are we still here?!" I let Dagger off his leash. He trotted over to Jacks, tail wagging, and licked his face.

Luke put his phone down. "Smith never came back to the bus last night."

"What? Why didn't anyone come get me?" I had one eye on Dags, making sure I didn't lose Lexi's dog. He lifted his leg and peed on the wheel closest to Jacks.

Jacks jumped up. "Not cool, bro!" Seemed he got some of Dagger's splatter.

Chase walked over. "When he didn't show up at eight, we didn't really think too much of it. It's happened before. But then when nine turned to ten…we went looking for him. We've called everyone we can think of, man. No one's seen him."

I pulled at my hair in frustration, "Again. Why the fuck didn't someone come get me?" I pulled out my phone.

Luke ground out, "We knew you were busy."

I took a step towards him, in that instant I wanted to hit him. He'd gone too far. "Don't start with me Luke. You should have woken me up the second he didn't show. And you know it."

Luke threw his hands in the air. "Why? Because you're the great and powerful Dash Conner and you can just conjure him out of thin air?"

"No, you ass wipe. Because I had a GPS tracker installed in his phone." I held up my phone, a map was showing with a blinking red dot signaling where Smith was.

Jacks came over and stared at my phone, then looked at me. "You put a tracker on him? That's kind of creepy dude. Do you have one on me?"

I handed my phone to Chase and motioned for Jacks to get back on the bus. "No, buddy, just Smith's. You know how irresponsible he can be."

I looked over at Luke. His eyebrows were raised in question. I just shrugged. Of course I had a tracker on Jacks's phone; he was just as bad as Smith. He didn't have Smith's penchant for uppers, but he did have other vices that got him in trouble. I heard Luke chuckle behind me. I wonder if he'd be laughing if he knew I had one installed on Lexi's phone yesterday?

"Hey, what's going on? Why are we still here?" Lex was sitting curled up on the couch, her laptop balanced on her legs.

Luke quickly sat down next to her before I could. Douche. "Smith never came back to the bus last night." He lay down and put his legs across Lexi's lap.

She just lifted her laptop and then set it down on Luke's legs. I hated how comfortable they were together, how natural it was for him to touch her, how she let him.

"My girlfriend's lap comfortable, Luke?" I resisted the urge to grab him and pull him off of her.

"Just as comfortable as it's always been, thanks for asking."

Without looking up from her computer Lexi reached over and pinched the inside of Luke's thigh. Although I didn't love seeing her hand that close to his dick, I liked the hissing sound he made. "Don't be an ass, Lukey."

Chase came from the front of the bus and handed me back my phone. "We have the address plugged in. He isn't too far from here. We'll scoop him up on our way out."

I checked my watch again. Yet another delay in getting Lexi that pill. We would be cutting it pretty damn close. Was the universe trying to tell us something? I glanced at my watch again, trying to do the math in my head.

Jacks threw an old french fry at my head. It bounced off and Dagger caught it in midair. "Why do you keep looking at your damn watch? What's the rush? We don't even play tonight. Calm down."

I looked up at Lexi. She was staring at me, lip caught in between her teeth. But not in a flirty way, in a worried way. "The big deal, jackass, is that Lexi's pill is waiting for us in Tennessee. And the closer it gets to 72 hours out, the less effective it is."

No one said anything after that. The next time I looked up to check on Lex though, she was looking at Luke.

Chase stuck his head around the corner, laughing. "We're here."

All four of us got up and peeked out the window. We were parked in front of a very unassuming apartment complex. It looked so damn ordinary; it was comical. I stood and put on a ball cap and my aviators. It was the best disguise I had at the moment. "I'll go get him."

Luke rose to his feet next to me. "I'll go. I'm still less recognizable than you are, man."

I shook my head. "Smith gets…let's just say 'down.' He might not come with you."

Luke glanced at Lexi before turning his eyes back towards me. "I know how to deal with bottomed out rockers, Dash."

"Still, it'll go faster if I do it. Just keep the bus running. I'll be in and out in no time." I grabbed my phone from Chase and hopped off the bus before anyone could try and stop me. The tracker I had was state of the art. It showed me the exact apartment number where Smith was. I climbed to the third floor of building four and knocked on the last door on the right. After a few seconds of silence, the door swung wide to reveal a pissed off looking dude. He was huge. Linebacker huge. "Uh, I'm looking for my buddy's phone. The tracker says it's here." Better to leave Smith's name unsaid until I knew what was what.

"I'm the only one here, man."

I looked around the brick wall of person standing in front of me. "You sure about that?" I held up my phone and showed him the blinking dot and his address.

He took a step back. "Check for yourself."

I walked in and quickly searched the living room and kitchen. There were empty cups everywhere and a floated keg in the corner. The place reeked worse than our tour bus after a bender. "Mind if I check the bedrooms?" Wouldn't put it past Smith to be in bed—with more than one girl.

"Be my guest. There isn't anyone here. The party got crazy after this rock star douche showed up. My neighbors called the cops around two a.m., and everyone fled."

The cops, no wonder this dude looked pissed off. And I could only imagine how irritating it had been when every girl in the room was throwing themselves at Smith. The bedroom was empty, but I found Smith's phone in the bathroom between the sink and the shower. I held it up to the angry giant. "Thanks, man. At least I found his phone."

The guy shrugged and shut the door as soon as I stepped out onto the landing. I hightailed it back to the bus. Luckily, there wasn't a crowd gathered around it—yet. We needed to get out of here though. I took off my ball cap as I shut and locked the door behind me. "Smith wasn't in there, just his phone." I tossed it to Jacks. "The guy that lives there said he had a party, but the cops were called and everyone left around two a.m. Smith was there at some point."

Luke leaned his head back against his seat and sighed, "Maybe he hit a bar after that?"

Lexi shook her head. "Bars around here close at one on Saturday."

Luke rolled his eyes. "And how would you know when the bars close around...? Oh, that's right...this isn't little Lexi's first trip to Starkville."

The smile Luke wore was making me want to punch him. I was already on edge. Smith was missing, Lexi needed to get to Tennessee and to her pill, and Luke was being smug about Lexi's past. A past that I not only wasn't part of, but didn't know about either. More memories for them to share. "Whatever. If he isn't at a bar then the only other place he could have gone was to another party."

Lexi frowned. "Hey maybe he just took a cab to a hotel and he's sleeping it off?"

Jacks started cracking up. "Oh Lexi, oh wow, you're hilarious. Ah, I needed a good laugh."

I sat down with my head in my hands. At this point we'd spent two more precious hours chasing after Smith. "Is it time to start calling hospitals?"

Luke ran his hands through his hair. "Doesn't sound like a bad idea."

"Hey y'all, wait. I think I found him." Jacks got up and came around to us, showing us something on Smith's phone. "That gossip site he follows, they just posted a picture of him that was supposedly taken around four a.m. this morning. It's from some chick's Twitter feed."

The picture was of Smith, surrounded by blonde, tanned co-eds. The group was standing in front of a fucking sorority house.

Chapter Eighteen

Lexi

A fucking sorority house? The last time I saw Smith he was entering a room full of girls that wanted to nail him. He left there, drank a shit ton and then spent the night at the sorority house we were currently parked in front of. Damn, Smith had stamina. "Is it wrong that I'm a little impressed?"

Luke and Dash both said yes at the same time. Jacks shrugged. "It is what it is. This is Smith and he's ours for better or worse." Wow, that was the most sentimental thing I had heard Jacks say. Granted I'd only know him for about four days, but still.

The large white house with pretentious columns was surrounded by people. There were college kids all over the lush green lawn. News was out that The Devil's Share was on campus. At least the paparazzi hadn't shown up yet. They were probably having trouble getting onto campus; plus we had driven through a maze to find this place.

Chase headed towards the door. "I'll go get him. Y'all stay here. We don't want to incite a riot having all of The Devil's Share seen coming out of a sorority house. The press will be here any second I'm sure."

I held my hand out to stop him. "No, let me go. You're a guy, you can't just walk into a sorority house unnoticed."

"No way, Lex. Those kids will swarm you as soon as you step off the bus. Plus, we have no idea what's going on in there, we have no idea how...we just don't know." I knew why Luke was protesting. He was having flashbacks of that night with Sam.

Dash must have known it too. "Luke, man, Smith isn't ever violent. I have seen him at his worst, and he still isn't that bad. I wouldn't let Lex go in there if I thought for one second she could get hurt. And Chase can walk her to the door, he can keep the people back."

Luke's eyes cut to mine. He narrowed them and shook his head. But he sat down in defeat. Now he knew that I'd told Dash about that night. I knew that Luke and I needed to have a talk...but now obviously wasn't the time. I slipped on my chucks that were still by the door from last night. I could pass for a college co-ed. My wet hair was braided to the side. I had on a t-shirt and some legging/sweatpants. Seemed like the right outfit after a night partying with a rock star. The walk to the front door wasn't as bad as I had expected. Some of the kids wandered over to the bus, but for the most part they just stood in place and gawked. I heard my name being murmured though. Dash was right, one little article from the press and I was a household name. The door to the house wasn't locked, not very smart for college girls. I walked in and closed the door behind me. I heard music coming from the room next to me. I recognized it instantly—Smith. He was strumming a guitar and singing softly, something slow, painful and hypnotic. He was surrounded by girls wearing teeny tiny shirts and even smaller shorts. I glanced down at what I was wearing. Huh, guess I didn't fit in after all. There must have been twenty girls sitting around him. They were all staring with stars in their eyes. It was like Smith had them in a trance. I leaned against the wall and waited for the song to finish. It was so beautiful; I didn't have the heart to interrupt him. When he was done I placed my hand on his head, rubbing lightly. "Hey, buddy."

Smith looked like hell. His eyes were bloodshot. He had dark circles under them. He looked pale and thin. His voice sounded forced and horse. "Hey, Lex. Is it time to go home now?"

"Yeah, bud, it's time to go home." I helped him to his feet. His whole body started to shake. "Is this your guitar?"

"No. I found it upstairs." I took the guitar from his trembling hands and set it over to the side. I could feel the girls' eyes on me. A few of them started to protest, to reach for Smith. Like he was their prize. A lot of the girls looked worse for the wear. Some had eyes that looked a lot like Smith's. Please God don't let him have given these girls drugs to take. Talk about bad publicity.

"Hey aren't you Alexis Grant? You're Dash Conner's girlfriend." Everyone started whispering and taking out their cell phones.

I took a deep breath and put an arm around Smith's waist; he wasn't very steady on his feet. I whispered in his ear, "They are going to take pictures of this, and they are going to sell them. Try and stand up straight and make it look like we are walking out as a couple and not like I'm carrying you out of here, okay? When I walked in there were no paparazzi, just more college kids on the front lawn."

He nodded and straightened as much as he could. It would be better for the world to think I was a whore than for the world to think The Devil's Share bassist was a fucking mess. It was slow going but I got him to the door. I turned around to face the group of girls. "Do not follow us. If you come out front, the band's managers are going to come in here and take your phones and make you sign non-disclosures. It'll be a mess. Just stay inside." I had no idea what would actually happen. I was pretty sure there weren't any lawyers or bigwig managers on the tour right now. But it worked. As soon as the door shut behind us Smith sagged against my body. "Okay buddy, if I'm going to get you across this yard and onto the bus, I'm going to need a little help." Chase came around his other side and helped me get him back on his feet. Dozens of cell phones were pointed at us. But again, thankfully, no one approached us.

"I'm really sorry, Lexi. Is everyone mad? Is Dash mad? He used the tracker didn't he?"

We were taking baby steps, but we were making progress. "Hey, no one is mad. We were all just so worried about you." I was lying; everyone was pissed. I just hoped they let him recover before they laid into him.

"I tried, Lexi. I tried to be good. But the groupies, it wasn't enough. And then the sorority…it wasn't enough. Nothing was making me forget. I needed something more. I'm so sorry. I usually don't even answer his calls, but I just wanted to make sure he was okay…."

His words made me sick to my stomach, but the sound of his voice tore at my heart. "Shhhh, it's okay, buddy." I assumed by "him" he meant Jared. From what Dash had told me, Jared was toxic. Once we made it to the bus, Chase left us to open the door. I felt Smith's knees buckle seconds before we went down. Jacks was the first one out of the bus to help us. Seemed like Jacks a soft spot in his heart for his band mate. He stood Smith up like he weighed nothing and all but dragged him the rest of the way. Dash came, scooped me up and carried me up the stairs. "Kitten, are you okay?"

I nodded. "I'm fine. Smith isn't though. Look can you and Luke just give him a break? Just let him recover before you rip him a new asshole. Please. Jared called him."

When we got on the bus Jacks dumped Smith on the couch. Dash put me down and then grabbed Luke's arm. "Hey, can I talk to you a minute?" Luke gave a quick nod and then followed Dash towards the back.

Dagger went up and licked Smith's hand and then lay down on the floor beside the couch. He knew his new friend wasn't doing great, dog intuition. I looked over at Jacks, his face was hard to read but when he caught me watching he walked into the bathroom and shut the door. Okay, great. Smith was on the couch, curled up in the fetal position and moaning. Well not really moaning, more like whimpering. I went to the bunk I had seen him sleeping in and grabbed his pillow and his blanket. The guys were going to throw a bitch fit about this. I lifted his head and sat down. I placed the pillow on my lap and laid his head on it. I covered us up with the blanket and began to rub his head. He turned towards my touch and stopped making that sad sound. Within a few minutes his breathing evened out. He was asleep. My eyes were starting to feel heavy too.

"Really, Lex?" Luke was standing over me, hands on his hip and a scowl on his face. "You really think he needs to be babied right now?"

"Shhhh! Don't wake him up. I just got him to calm down." I winked trying to lighten the mood, knowing I wasn't doing anything but proving that I was in fact babying him.

Dash came in the room. I steeled myself for his reaction. To my surprise he simply leaned down and kissed my forehead before settling on the floor against my legs. He constantly surprised me. "Where's Jacks?" At the sound of his name, Jacks walked out of the bathroom. He was carrying a wet washcloth, which he placed on Smith's forehead.

I cleared my throat. "He needs to see a doctor, y'all."

Jacks shook his head. "Nah, he's fine. I've seen him worse off than this."

I nodded. "Exactly. You've seen him worse. Smith has no doubt put his body through the paces the last few years. How do you know he'll bounce back this time? He was so out of it, so frail. He's clammy and whimpering. I'm sure you guys can pay someone to come out here and check on him. Make sure he's okay before we hit the road again."

Dash kneeled down in front of me. "Lex, we need to get to Tennessee. Smith will be fine."

"You don't know that. Look, just call a doctor to check him out. Another hour isn't going to make that big of a difference, right? My pill is there waiting for us."

Seconds later Smith's shakes came back with vengeance and the guys conceded and called a doctor. It ended up taking an hour for him to get to us and then another hour for him to hook Smith up to some IV fluids and check his vitals. In the end? He was fine. Well, as fine as he could be when he'd come dangerously close to ODing. After the doctor left, we hit the road, and everyone settled in for the long ride.

Luke handed Jacks an Xbox controller before sitting down and leaning back in the recliner. Dagger put his head in Dash's lap and Jacks lay down on the floor with his head on Dagger's side and his feet up on the recliner next to Luke's. We were all touching; we were all connected. No matter how irritated or worried or mad or nervous any of us were, we were in this together. My heart swelled and tears filled my eyes. These guys, in the blink of an eye, had just become my whole world.

***

"Lexi? Lex. Wake up, sweet girl." I opened my eyes and sat up. At some point I'd fallen asleep and fallen over onto Smith. "Sorry, I just really need to piss." Smith got up and swayed on his way to the bathroom, using walls and doorframes to keep from falling over, dragging his IV pole behind him.

I was alone until he came back. "Where is everyone?"

Smith gestured behind us to the window. "We stopped for food I think." Smith was wringing his hands together and bouncing his leg up and down. "Lexi, I'm really sorry that you had to come get me. I don't normally...I mean I do, but I haven't used in a long time. Not since Jared left."

I could play this a couple of ways. I could tell him it was all okay and we were all just glad that he was safe, which is the same crap I fed him when I went in to drag him out of the sorority house, or... "What you did Smith? It's not okay. So many terrible things could have happened and you would have had no memory or no control. A house full of college girls? My God, Smith. Think of the possibilities. Think of the headlines. Think of the band. Your actions could have ruined this for everyone involved. And not just the guys, y'all have employees. You have people who count on you. What you did was selfish." Up until this point Smith hadn't looked at me once. He kept his eyes trained on his hands. I leaned down and put my face next to his, making him look me in the eye. "If you feel like you can't handle something, or you feel lost or like you need an escape and the girls aren't working, you come find us. No matter what time it is, no matter what else is going on, you come find us. We are all here for you, Smith."

He nodded, "Yeah, okay. I will. I promise I'll try harder."

I curled my legs underneath me. "What did you take?"

"Too much coke followed by too much Xanax. I swear that's all I took. No heroin, no speedballs. My tolerance is just so low and—" The door to the bus opened cutting Smith off.

"Hey, look who's up." Jacks came and sat down on the other side of Smith and handed him a huge sandwich. "Lots of ham, hold the mayo."

Dash handed me one too. "Good thing Luke has your incredibly specific sub sandwich order memorized." He rolled his eyes and sat on the floor.

Luke puffed out his chest. "What can I say? After all these years I've become an expert in all things Lexi."

Dash chuckled, "Not *all* things man. There's a lot of Lexi that you have no knowledge of." He winked at me. "If you know what I'm saying."

Luke flicked him on the ear and then raced into the bathroom and shut the door.

Chapter Nineteen

Dash

We were finally at the hotel. I was so freaking happy to be getting off that bus. We'd get Lex her pill and then she and I were spending the rest of the night locked away in our suite. Hotels were a luxury on the road; we were rarely in one place long enough to justify staying off the bus. Chase came over and handed out our keys. "Here you go boys, enjoy. Sound check is tomorrow at noon. I'm going to go crash, but call me if you need anything. I'll keep my phone on." Chase pulled me to the side and handed me a brown paper bag. "Here's Lexi's pill."

"I owe you man. I really do. Thank you." I opened the bag and tore the foil packet holding the pill. I stuffed the bag way down in the lobby trashcan. Lex was standing in the bar laughing with Jacks and Luke. She looked so damn pretty, her hair wavy from the way it dried in her braid. She'd put on some ripped jeans and wife beater with a sweater. She never even tried to be beautiful; she just was. I handed her the pill and a bottle of water. "Bottoms up, Kitten." She stared at the pill for a second before she took it and then handed me back the bottle of water, smiling.

Jacks started clapping. "Yeah! Glad that's over. Now Dash can stop obsessive compulsively checking his watch."

Luke chuckled, "I for one am tired of watching his brain smoke while he tries to count down the hours in his head."

I put my arm around Lexi. I was too happy to be irritated with the teasing. I had my girl, her dog, and a hotel room. Life was good. Speaking of the hundred pound pit bull, we needed to get him up to the room soon; he was definitely drawing attention to us. The hotel was mostly deserted at this hour, but everyone around was staring. Smith slid into a nearby booth. "One drink and then we all go our separate ways for our night off."

"All right. One drink." As much as I wanted to get Lex upstairs, I knew Smith needed this. He needed to know we were all over the drama from this morning and we all still loved him.

One drink turned into two before I was able to pull Lexi out of the booth. "We're out of here. We'll see you guys at sound check." I took her hand in mine and got Dagger out from under the booth where he was asleep.

"Hey leave Dags with me? If that's okay?" Smith was looking at Lexi, eyes pleading. He didn't want to be alone tonight, and he didn't want to go look for a destructive distraction. Progress? Or a monster hangover?

Lexi smiled and took the leash from me, handing it to Smith. "Of course, buddy. I fed him before we got off the bus. He'll just need one more walk before bed and some water." Smith nodded.

A young guy wearing a Devil's Share t-shirt walked up to the table holding a tray of shots. "Excuse me, but I'm a huge fan. Do you think I could get your autographs? I brought Jäger."

Oh fuck. I turned to push Lexi back, but it was too late. She was already gagging with her hand over her mouth. I got eye level with her. "Kitten, look at me. Just calm down. Calm down. Breath through your mouth. Deep breathes. Please don't throw up that pill, baby." I took deep breaths, trying to get her breathing to calm down and match mine.

She nodded and closed her eyes, breathing through her mouth so she didn't smell the alcohol. After a few seconds she opened her eyes. "Okay. Okay. I think I'm okay. That was close." She stepped around me. "Goodnight, guys."

She bent down to pet Dagger the same time the kid with the tray of Jäger went to set it on the table. They collided and the shots spilled all over the table and Lexi's shirt. The licorice-sweet smell of Jäger filled the air. Mother fucker. I covered my eyes and let my head fall back. The next sound I heard was Lexi throwing up. Smith started to gag. Vomit made him gag. Jacks grabbed a straw and started sucking the spilled Jäger off the table. Luke banged his head on the wall.

Lexi stood up and wiped her mouth with the back of her hand. She had tears in her eyes. "I'm so sorry. I—"

"Hey, don't be sorry, Kitten. This isn't your fault. It's no one's fault, okay?" Except for the dumb ass fan.

Luke stood up. "Maybe it's okay. Maybe she already digested it." He peered over the table. Wow, Luke really did love Lexi. He was checking her vomit. "Nope. Not okay." He looked at me. "Sorry, man, she threw up the pill. Wellllll, part of the pill anyway." Luke looked up at Lexi. "Lexi just pick it up and wash it off. Hurry, before your acidic puke dissolves it."

Now I wanted to vomit. Lexi groaned and made a move to pick up what was left of the pill. She almost made it too. But Dagger was too fast. And he was a dog, you couldn't really blame him. Dogs like vomit.

***

Lexi was sitting in the hot bubble bath I'd drawn for her. I wanted to join her, and I planned on joining her. But I had to step into the other room and freak out for a second. How did I feel about this? How did Lexi feel? Would she hate me for putting her in this situation? Would she leave me? Oddly enough I wasn't freaking out about the possibility of a baby, I was freaking over the thought of losing Lex. I was pacing, pulling at my hair, and punching the air. I even did a few ninja air kicks; I'm not ashamed.

"Dash, will you please stop assaulting the air and come in here?" *How does she always know when I'm doing that?*

I smoothed my hair, took a deep breath, and opened the bathroom door. "I was just calling room service, Kitten. No worries." She gave me her withering look. It wasn't a total lie. I had called room service. I got naked and climbed in the giant tub behind her. She leaned back against my chest.

"We need to talk about this." Her body looked so good wet and covered in bubbles. I ran my fingers down her arms and across her chest, leaving a trail of suds in my wake. "We tried to be responsible adults and an accident happened. We tried to fix it and the universe told us to fuck off. Now we just wait and see what happens."

"Dash, I…uh I don't really know how to say this." She sat up and turned to face me. "I had no problem taking the pill. I mean, no moral issues with it I guess. But if I'm pregnant, I can't…I won't…"

I put my hand over her mouth. "It's okay Lex, I get it. I agree, wholeheartedly. If there's a baby, then we're having a baby. We'll figure it out."

She nipped at my fingers with her straight white teeth making my dick twitch. "Dash, please understand, I don't want to trap you into anything. I could do it on my own. You don't have to do anything you don't want to here."

My stomach dropped. Is that what she thought of me? "Look,
Kitten. I'm not going anywhere. Sure, rock and roll is not the right
lifestyle for a baby. When we aren't touring, we're writing. When
we aren't writing, we're recording. It's nonstop. And it'll be that
way for a few more years, at least. But we won't be able to do this
forever. This life won't last. And I would never turn away from my
child. Ever." I turned her around and pulled her back against my
chest. I placed both my hands on her stomach. "I'm here. For
whatever comes next, I'm here." I placed a kiss on her neck, then her
cheek. She turned her head and her mouth met mine. I ran my tongue
along the seam of her lips, asking to be let in. She opened for me.
She tasted like the vodka she'd been drinking earlier, so good. She
turned in my arms and climbed on my lap. There was nothing
between us but the water, nothing stopping me from taking her. I
pulled back and held her face in my eyes, studying her.

Lexi gave me a little smile and a shrug. "Why the hell not?"

I entered her tight little body, kissing her with everything I had.
My hands trailed down her back as she rode my dick. My head fell
back against the edge of the bathtub and water started to slosh over
the side. "You feel so fucking good, Kitten. It's never been like this
before, Lexi." I'm sure she thought I meant the sex, but I meant so
much more.

***

After the day we'd had, the bathtub sex, the room service, and
the hotel bed sex, you'd think I would have crashed the second my
head hit the pillow. But I was lying awake, holding Lexi close to me,
and staring out the floor to ceiling window. I had pulled the curtains
back so we could see the night skyline. It had made for an incredibly
romantic backdrop. My phone vibrated on the nightstand. I reached
over and rolled my eyes when I saw the picture flashing behind
Luke's name. The douche had made his contact picture a selfie of
him and Lexi—he was kissing her cheek and she was just making a
kissy face. "Nice picture, man."

Luke chuckled, "I thought you'd like that."

"It's late. Is everything okay? Smith and Jacks good?" I worried
about my band mates, always. Unless they were with me, I worried
about them. Huh, kind of like a parent, right? Maybe I could do this.

"Yeah, everyone is fine. I made sure they were both in their rooms before I headed to mine. I was calling to check on you guys, to check on Lex."

I looked down at the girl sleeping soundly in my arms and couldn't help but smile. "We're good, man. Thanks."

Luke cleared his throat. "What are you...what are y'all going to do. I mean...what now?"

He was treading lightly, making sure he didn't over step his boundaries. This was a first for Luke when it came to Lexi. "Uh, well, we're just going to wait and see what happens. If she's...if we...if there's a baby, then we're having a baby. I guess we'll know in a couple of weeks."

"Whatever happens, Dash, when it comes to Lex, I'll always be here. For whatever she needs as long as she needs it." I knew what he was saying, if I screwed this up then he would be there to pick up the pieces. Luke would have no problems raising my kid as if it was his own. As long it was part Lexi, he'd love it.

"I hear ya, man. But, I'm not going anywhere. No matter what happens, I'm not going anywhere."

Chapter Twenty

Lexi

"Do I really have to wake up?"

"Yes, Kitten. I don't know if you remember this but you are supposed to be taking pictures of us for our next album. So if we're at sound check, you need to be at sound check." He slapped my ass.

"Slave. Driver." I rolled out of bed, naked, and walked across the room to the closet to find some clothes. Just like I predicted Dash came up behind me and started kissing my neck. I leaned to the side giving him better access. "Maybe you aren't so bad after all."

***

I'd never been to sound check in a big arena. All of Luke's sound checks with his old band had taken like ten minutes and were done while the crowd was waiting for them to go on. I snapped a picture of Dagger with his sound canceling headphones on. He was lying on the cement floor with his head resting on Smith's guitar case. I took a picture of Jacks sitting on the edge of the stage, feet dangling. Luke twirling his drum sticks while blowing a giant blue bubble with his gum. And Dash while he sang into his microphone staring right at me, smiling my favorite crooked grin. All the men in my life, immortalized in pictures.

"Hey, Lexi."

My blood ran cold. I'd recognize that voice anywhere. I turned and sneered, "What in the holy hell are you doing here?"

"Lex!" Luke was standing behind his drums, pointing his stick at me. "Play nice until I'm done here, please. I'm begging you."

I rolled my eyes and turned back to one of my least favorite people in the world. "Lacey, it's been a long time. Not nearly long enough, but a long time none the less." I snapped a picture of Luke's worried face. "Why are you here?"

The bitch giggled, "Lukey invited me."

"If you call him Lukey one more time, I'll cut you." I meant it.

Lacey nodded. "I can see you haven't changed one bit, Lexi." She studied her blood red nails. "Look, I'm not here to fight. I'm in town on business. I heard Luke was playing tonight and I just wanted to see him."

I scoffed, "You mean, now that he's famous, you wanted to see him."

She shook her head. "No, Lex. I just wanted to catch up with an old friend, plain and simple."

I kept my mouth shut for the rest of the sound check. Luke had asked me to play nice, nothing I had to say to Lacey Tyler would be nice. Lacey and Luke had dated on and off for a couple of years. Things would always start out great, but then she'd end up fucking him over. One time she just stopped talking to him, stopped taking his calls, and ignored him until he gave up. One time she told him that she couldn't be with someone with no future ahead of them, tried to make him choose between her or his music. One time, the last time, he'd walked in on her nailing one of his band mates. I was there for that one. It was towards the end of the tour that had gone to hell and Lacey's actions were just the icing on the cake. Lacey was bad news for Luke. I knew it. He knew it. Everyone fucking knew it. But she always seemed to lure him back in. Not this time, not if I had any damn say in it. I smiled to myself as I pulled out my phone to text Amy.

Me: The bitch is back.

If anyone hated Lacey more than I did, it was Amy. My phone vibrated in my hand.

Amy: WHAT?! Good thing you're there to shut that shit down. Let me know if you need any help. Love you/hate you.

I laughed and put my phone back in my pocket. A few minutes later sound check was over and the guys climbed off the stage. I took Dagger's headphones off and slipped them into their case. Dash came over and slung his arm around my neck, pulling me against him and kissing my cheek loudly. "Kitten who's your friend?"

I laughed humorlessly. "She's not my friend. This is Luke's EX-girlfriend, Lacey Tyler. Lacy, this is my boyfriend, Dash Conner." I loved that I got to call him my boyfriend. I loved the look on Lacey's face when I said it. I pointed to Jacks and Smith in turn, introducing them. I looked over at Lacey. "Be careful not to accidentally blow them, okay?" She narrowed her eyes but said nothing. She knew she deserved it.

Luke finally made his way over to us. "Lexi, I heard that. Didn't I ask you to be nice?"

I shrugged. Luke had to know what my reaction would be to him inviting her here. Dash pulled me into his lap wrapping his arms around my middle. "Kitten's got claws." Then he whispered, "It's kind of turning me on." I snorted.

Luke took a deep breath. "Lacey and I were going to head back to the hotel to grab lunch. They have a nice rooftop bar. Do you guys want to come? I mean, you don't have to."

I said, "No." At the same time Jacks, Smith, and Dash said yes. I turned to look back at Dash. "Come on, I don't wanna. If we go back to the hotel...I'll play very nice with you." I used the same words I'd used a couple nights ago, hoping they would trigger a pleasant memory and get me out of lunch with Satan's sister.

Dash chuckled, "Oh I know you will, baby." He kissed my neck. "But watching Luke's anxiety level rise at the thought of you two girls sharing a meal is too damn tempting to pass up."

***

The restaurant was really pretty; everything was clean modern lines and glass. We had a spectacular view of the skyline. The sun was warm but not too warm. The hostess had seated us at a long rectangular table and was waiting patiently to take our drink orders.

Dash smiled up at the young girl and she blushed. "I'll have a whiskey and coke, and she'll have a...uh...a water."

I laughed, "I'll have a vodka and soda, lot's of lime please." I felt Dash stiffen at my side. "What?"

Dash looked down the table, everyone instantly turned away like they hadn't been watching us. He held his menu up and talked behind it. "Lex, what if you *are* pregnant?"

Dash was taking the role of maybe baby daddy a little too far. I took a very deep, very controlled breath and grabbed the hostess before she left. "Can I change my order to a glass of Prosecco, please?"

"Yes, ma'am."

I turned to Dash, eyebrows raised. "Better?"

Dash shrugged and then talked out the side of his mouth, "To be honest, I rather you not drink at all, babe."

I smiled tightly and replied in a singsong voice, "If I don't drink for the next two weeks, then neither do you."

He smiled up at the hostess. "The Prosecco will be fine, thank you."

Smith hid his chuckle behind his hand. Guess we hadn't been as secretive as we thought. I looked down and across from me at Lacey to see if she had heard anything. But all her attention was focused on Luke. Gross. "So Lacey, you said you were here on business. Is your pimp setting up out of town gigs for you now?"

Luke scrubbed his hands down his face. "For the love of God, Lex, could—"

Lacey put her hand on his arm, silencing him. "Luke, it's okay. We both know why Lexi feels the way she does about me. I was horrible to you, and I deserve her anger." She looked at me. "I was young and selfish and cruel. I regret the way I treated Luke, and I regret that you were there to witness my immature behavior. I'm just here to catch up with an old friend."

Stupid bitch took all the wind out of my sails. I inwardly rolled my eyes, and gave her a small smile. "Are you still with that marketing firm in Dallas?"

Some of the tension left Luke's body. Lacey nodded. "I am. I actually just got a pretty big promotion, which is why I'm traveling so much right now. Luke tells me that you are doing the pictures for the band's next album? I'd love to see what you've got so far. You've always had such a great eye."

So this was going to be our new relationship? Pleasantries and small talk? Boo. I liked her better when she was throwing insults my way and letting busboys take body shots out of her belly button. At one time, Lacey and I had been friends. At one time, we used to have a lot fun together.

Lunch went by without another hitch. Dagger was lying under the table at Dash and my feet. I was pretty sure dogs weren't allowed in this restaurant let alone this hotel. Being with the band definitely had its perks. Jacks put his hand under the table and fed Dags a piece of bacon. "Can I have Dags tonight?"

"If you want, but don't you have *female* roommates lined up?" I drank the last of my Prosecco. I had made it last because I was pretty sure trying to order another one would have meant a second behind-the-menu discussion with Dash.

Jacks chuckled, "Oh silly Lexi. I never bring girls back to my hotel room. Hotels are meant for relaxing and recharging. I'll just get someone to blow me backstage before I head home."

It was semi-depressing that his words didn't elicit any shock or awe. It simply was my life on the road with The Devil's Share. I pursed my lips and nodded. "Okay, just come by our room and pick him up when you get back."

Smith leaned back in his chair, put his hands behind his head and spoke to Jacks, "Think I can bunk with you tonight?" My heart went out to him. He still didn't want to be alone and Jacks had just commandeered his furry roommate.

"Sure, man." Jacks held up his hand for a high five. "It'll be just like old times, when we were too poor to have separate rooms on tour."

Dash stood and reached for my hand. "We will see you guys at the venue." We stopped off at the end of the table to say good-bye to Luke and Lacey. "Lacey, you should ride to the venue with Luke. You can hang backstage with Lex and watch the show from the side stage."

I squeezed the ever-loving hell out of Dash's hand. He didn't even flinch. So I sucked it up. "Yeah, come with Luke. It'll be nice to catch up." And by nice, I meant that I would grill her until she caved and told me why she was really here.

Chapter Twenty-One

Dash

I took another sip of my whiskey as I watch Lexi get dressed. Just watching her do something as simple as button her pants turned me on. I could have this girl a hundred times a day and it still wouldn't be enough. She was wearing this dark red flowy top with some leather leggings and sky-high heels. Her hair was wavy down her back and her eyes were lined and smoky. She looked lethal. She walked over to me and grabbed the glass out of my hand taking a small sip, daring me to say something. I shook my finger at her and took my drink back. "No, Kitten."

She rolled her eyes. "I think you are being a little too protective, Dash."

I pulled her closer to me, placing my hand on her tiny stomach. "No such thing as too protective if my little baby is in there." I kissed her neck. "Is it odd that we've done a complete one-eighty? We went from chasing down the morning after pill, to discussing this possible baby with a smile on our faces."

Lex shrugged. "I don't know. I guess it is a pretty big about-face. But what else should we do? We made a choice about what we were comfortable with and what we weren't. If there's a baby, I'm good. If not, that's okay too. We're both successful adults. We can afford to give a child a great life. I've always known I wanted to have a baby at some point. Why not be happy about the possibility?"

"Is it weird that it totally turns me on?"

She placed her hand over mine and laughed. "What does? Telling me what to do?" She tried to take my glass again. I handed her the glass of white wine I'd poured her earlier.

"No. The thought that my baby might be in there. I know it sounds crazy, but ever since last night… Just thinking that I did that, well, that I might have done that…I don't know, it's hot." I grabbed the back of her neck and pulled her mouth against mine. Our tongues swirled and danced. I put my drink down behind me and wrapped my arms around her waist, running my hands down her tight little ass. "You are so damn sexy, Kitten." I went back in for another kiss but stopped when I heard my phone ring. I groaned, "Yeah?"

"Mr. Conner, sir, your car is waiting down stairs."

"Okay. Thank you." I put my phone back in my pocket. "It's time to go." I grabbed Dagger's leash and put my hand on the small of Lexi's back guiding her to the door.

When we were in the elevator I felt her press against me as she whispered in my ear, "It turns me on too." She took my earlobe in her mouth. "I can't explain it. But the thought that you could own and possess my body so fully that we created a baby...it's hot." My whole body broke out in goose bumps. My dick was hard as a fucking rock. There was no way I could wait until after the show to have her. When the elevator door opened to the lobby, I pressed the door close button and then the button to our floor. I took out my phone. "Tell our driver that we're going to be running a little late."

***

By the time we made it back downstairs and into the car, we were running more than a little late. Not so late that the show would be delayed, but late enough that my band mates would notice and give me crap for it. I put my hand between Lexi's thighs and leaned back in the seat, savoring my last few minutes of peace and quiet for next three hours.

"You know, I'm not really pumped about having to hang out backstage with Lacey, so thanks for that."

There went my few minutes of peace. "I know you aren't, Kitten. But if you want Luke to trust in your decision to be with me, then maybe you should try and trust his decision to hang out with Lacey for a couple of days."

"No I shouldn't. She's a stupid whore."

I chuckled, "So was I." She gave me an irritated eye roll. "Did you ever stop to think that maybe just a small piece of your anger is actually jealousy?" Oops. As the words were leaving my mouth I wanted to reach out and grab them and stuff them back in. I meant it, Lexi was used to being the center of Luke's universe. Who would want to share that spotlight? But I should have just kept my mouth shut.

Lexi's fists clenched; her eyes narrowed. At least she didn't make me move my hand. "Are you freaking kidding me, Dash Conner?! Jealousy?! Lacey has proven over and over again that she can't be trusted, that she'll cheat and manipulate and lie to get her way. Every time she comes back, he ends up letting her back in. And then she ruins him. Destroys him. She's like a drug. Lacey is Luke's heroin."

"Kitten, I—"

She held her hand up. "Nope. No more talking. For the rest of this car ride, I get to be mad at you."

Only, the rest of the car ride? That wasn't so bad, that meant I'd still get a kiss before I went on stage tonight. Plus, I'd get my quiet time. Man, I was smitten with this girl. Even her anger was somewhat pleasant. When we got to the venue we were ushered inside through the back way and then into the dressing room with the rest of the band, plus Lacey-the-illicit-drug.

Luke looked up when we walked in. "Nice of you guys to finally grace us with your presence."

Lexi pointed at Luke. "Shut it."

Smith chuckled, "Wow Lex, mood swings kicking in already?"

She whirled on him next. "Don't you even think about starting with me, Sorority Row."

Obviously her bad mood didn't end in the car. I laughed; I couldn't help it. She was adorable when she was mad. Like a fallen angel. "Kitten, if you're mad at me, take it out on me. Don't stress the whole band out before we have to go on." I walked over to the bar and poured her a glass of wine. She hadn't finished her glass at the hotel. I figured a few glasses a night, until we knew for sure, would keep us both happy. I crooked my finger at her, holding the glass out and giving her the smile I knew she loved.

She walked over to me, took a big sip and then a deep cleansing breath. "See what you did?"

I held my hands up in surrender. "Hey, I thought your anger ended in the car." I slipped my hands around her waist and nuzzled her neck. "Come on, Kitten. I need a little lovin' before I go make the money that'll keep you in pregnancy couture." She snorted against my shoulder, but I could feel her smile. She finally relented and put her arms around me, holding me tight. Just like that, our first fight was over. And I suddenly wanted to cancel the show and go back to our room and find out what make-up sex with Lexi would be like.

There was a knock on the door. "It's go time, guys." We had a rule: if it was time to go on, they told us through the door. We didn't like strangers invading our space before a show.

I pulled away from Lexi's body and held her face in my hands. "Be nice, Kitten. Please, for me."

She nodded. "I promise. Go rock their world." She gestured in the direction of the stage.

"You're coming with me. I hated not seeing you during our last show. No more backstage for you." I took her hand and grabbed Dagger's headphone case as I headed towards the door. Dagger didn't even require a leash anymore. He knew the drill. I placed the headphones on his head and gave him the leave-it command. I grabbed Lexi, kissing her deeply one more time. I stepped out on stage, and just like always, the crowd went fucking wild.

Chapter Twenty-Two

Lexi

The show was spectacular, per usual. The only downside was the fact that Lacey Tyler was standing next to me. She kept looking over at me every few seconds. I knew she had something to say, but I kept ignoring her. Everyone kept instructing me to be nice, and just like earlier, if I was to be nice I couldn't talk.

She kneeled down and pet Dagger. "He's a beautiful dog, Lex. How long have you had him?"

I rolled my eyes. Trying to get in my good graces by complimenting my badass dog? Lame. "About two years."

"He's so good, so behaved."

I did chuckle at that. "His good behavior is a new development. He was a destructive mess before he met the band. Sometimes I wonder if he knows that they are mess enough for all of us, and leaves the job to them."

Lacey stood and shrugged. "Maybe he just grew up and realized the error of his ways."

"Look, if you think—"

She held up her hand and shook her head. "Please Lex, just hear me out." I took a deep breath, but remained quiet. "I know you don't like me, and I get it. When I think of the way I treated Luke, it makes me sick. But I can't say this enough, I am here to make amends. I wanted to apologize to Luke, that's all. I mean come on, Lex, we were so young. You can't tell me that there isn't anything you regret, anything you would change if given the chance."

I cocked my head to the side, studying her. Her words rang true. We'd all done stupid shit that could just be chalked up to immaturity. Maybe Dash was right. Maybe I should just trust Luke's judgment. He wasn't the same kid he used to be either. "Fine. We can call a truce. But I swear to everything holy, if you hurt him in any way…I'll end you."

Lacey smiled like the cat that ate the canary. "Fair enough." This girl couldn't be truthful to save her pathetic little life.

Dash looked over at me and winked. I swooned (yet again). I'd never get enough of him doing that in front of a sold-out crowd.

People out there were chanting his name, singing along to his songs. And he was thinking about me.

"So, you and Dash?"

"Me and Dash." I tried to control my smile, but my face won.

"I'm not trying to pry, but none of you guys are very subtle with the jokes and innuendos. Are you pregnant?"

I shifted on my feet, not sure how to answer her. "Nope." Telling that lie hurt, in a very odd way. I felt like I was betraying my kid, or my heart. But I'd be damned if I let Lacey alert the press to this…situation.

"Oh, well, it just seemed like—"

"Yeah, the guys have weird sense of humor. It's just a running joke." I bit my lip to keep from smiling. Up until this exact moment, I wasn't sure if I should let myself be excited about the idea of having a baby. But now I knew, my initial reaction when asked was joy. And the fact that I couldn't share my joy was making me hate her even more.

Jacks's voice came over the sound system, my eyes flew to the stage. He rarely if ever talked during the shows. "So I know Dash has been going on and on about his girlfriend this past week. We all know he's smitten." Jacks looked over at me and chuckled, "He's a smitten kitten." Dash threw his head back and laughed at Jacks's use of my nickname. "But I have a new love too." The crowd started cheering. He used his hands to quiet them back down. "Well, actually I think Smith and I are kind of sharing our new crush." The crowd went wild again as Jacks winked. "Wanna meet 'em?"

I shook my head as I leaned down and put on Dagger's leash. Jacks jogged over to the side of the stage and I handed him the leash. "You are a nut."

He laughed. "I know. But I love this guy. He's part of the band. He needs to be introduced to our world."

I watched as Jacks led Dags out on to the stage. Smith came over and gave him a good scratch behind the ears. The crowd and the lights didn't seem to bother Dagger in the least. He sat there between Jacks and Smith and soaked up the attention.

Chapter Twenty-Three

Dash

Lexi and I were lying in bed, as naked as the day we were born. I was trailing my fingers lightly over her flat stomach. "I wonder what's going on in there?"

Lex threaded her fingers through my hair, pulling slightly. "You guys are going to have to be more careful about the knocked up jokes. Lacey asked me if I was pregnant."

I looked up at her, eyes wide. "Well since she was still standing at the end of the show, I take it you two made up?"

She laughed, "Made up? No, sir. More like called a temporary truce. She assured me that she came to apologize to Luke and catch up. Now that's done and over and I can go back to hating her."

I resumed my stomach drawings. I didn't want to burst Lexi's bubble, but I was almost positive that Lacy hadn't left after the show. Luke rarely hooked up with groupies; it just wasn't his thing. But a hot ex-girlfriend? He'd hit that all night. As long as he got her out of this hotel before we had to get on the bus in the morning, he'd be golden. Let Lexi catch him? The shit would hit the fan. "What did you tell Lacey? When she asked about our maybe baby?"

"I told her that y'all just had a weird sense of humor. I don't trust her. I couldn't tell her I might be pregnant."

"If someone you loved or trusted asked you, what would you say?" I knew what I'd say. I knew how I felt at this point. But sometimes Lex was hard to read.

She put her hand on top of mine on her stomach. "I'd tell them the truth, that I'm actually pretty excited."

I could hear the smile in her voice. I moved back up the bed before pulling her body against mine. Our talk last night in the bathtub…that moment had changed my life forever. I couldn't help my smile any more than she could help hers, "I am too, Kitten." I rolled her body on top of mine. She knew exactly what I wanted. She lowered her body onto my cock, always ready for me, taking me inside of her as far I could go. She threw her head back and let out a little moan. I closed my eyes and ran my hands along her thighs. Lexi began to ride me at a sinfully slow pace. Everything about sex with her was decadent, too good to be true. The closer she got to an orgasm the harder and faster her movements became. I sat up, wrapping my hands around her shoulders as leverage to pull her down onto me deeper. "Baby, you feel so fucking good." I let my hand come between us and trail up her body. I placed my hand at the base of her throat, angling her body away from mine just enough to give her what she needed. "Come for me, Lexi." And she did.

***

The next morning after taking a shower together, where we got very dirty before we got clean, we headed down stairs. The bus was all packed, loaded, and ready to go.

Lexi went to climb up the steps but stopped short. "Are you freaking kidding me?!"

I followed her gaze. We all watched as Lacey kissed Luke and then got into a cab. I mumbled, "Dammit Luke." He almost got away with it and the rest of us almost got away without having to hear Lexi scream at him for the rest of the day. "Lex, you can't cause a scene in the parking lot, just get on the bus. Please." By the grace of God she did what I asked.

Jacks headed straight for the bathroom, no doubt locking himself in with his PS3 until the storm blew over. Smart bastard.

Smith got down on his knees at Lexi's feet. "Please Mommy, don't yell at Uncle Luke." He stood. "It's bad for my sobriety."

She popped him on the back of the head and then headed down the hall to our room. She came out carrying Dagger's noise-canceling headphones. I chuckled as I watched her put them on Smith. I sat down on the couch, arms crossed, waiting for her to explode.

The instant Luke stepped on the bus, Lexi let him have it. "Please tell me you did not do something as asinine as bang Lacey?! You are better than that!"

Luke rolled his eyes. "What? You can sleep with Dash. Smith and Jacks can screw their way across the United States? But I can't hook up with an ex-girlfriend? Why do I have to sleep alone every fucking night?"

"You don't have to sleep alone. You just can't sleep with her! Lacey?! Lacey?! She's a whore, Luke!"

"So is he!" Luke pointed at me.

I raised my hands. "Hey! Not cool man." I was a reformed whore. But they both just kept screaming at each other like I hadn't even said anything.

Lexi put her hands on her hips. "It's not the same thing, Luke, and you damn well know it. Dash has been nothing but amazing to me. Lacey has lied to you, mind fucked you, and cheated on you."

"Oh so you don't want me, so no one can have me? That's pretty fucked up, Lex."

Lexi gave Luke a glare that could wither a plant. "What in the hell are you even talking about?! You're my family, Luke. I love you like a brother. Lacey?! She sure as hell doesn't give a shit out you!"

"She was a kid, Lex! So was I, and so were you. We're all different people now. We grew up."

"Yeah, we grew up. We let go of the destructive people in our lives!"

Luke ran his fingers through his hair. "Look, I'm not saying she's going to become a fixture around here, but we're friends. I know you're only trying to protect me—" He collapsed on the couch and pulled Lexi onto his lap.

"Uh, I'm not really okay with my girlfriend sitting on your lap, dude." They both ignored me again. It was like I wasn't even in the damn room.

"—and when I give you and Dash a hard time, it's just because I'm trying to protect you. It has been me and you taking care of each other for so long, I don't think we even know any other way."

Lexi sighed. "You're right. Ever since that night, ever since that tour, we've been constantly trying to save each other. But we aren't kids anymore. We aren't making the same mistakes we used to." She leaned her head on his shoulder. "I'll try and keep my mouth shut about your whores."

Luke nodded solemnly. "And I'll try and keep my mouth shut about yours."

I raised my hand. "If I could interject y'all's little therapy session here…none of this is because you're secretly in love with my girlfriend, right?"

Luke rolled his eyes and rested his forehead against Lexi's. "I love her. But I'm not in love with her." His words were exactly what I wanted to hear, but his tone was all wrong. He sounded sad and lost.

I stood up. "Okay, that's enough. Lexi get off of Luke's lap before I punch him. Luke, stop calling me a whore. I resent it. I accept it, but I resent it." I walked over to the bathroom and pounded on the door. "Jacky Boy you can come out now. They're done screaming." I went and sat down on the couch and pulled Lexi against my side wrapping my arms all the way around her.

Luke laughed, "Jealous much?"

I held up my finger and thumb. "I'm this close Luke, this close. You call me a whore and paw all over my girlfriend?"

Jacks came in and took his usual spot on the floor next to Dagger. "I think group therapy would be very beneficial for all of us."

Chapter Twenty-Four

Dash

The next two weeks flew by. We played show after show, and Lexi was side stage for every one of them. I loved looking over and seeing her watch me perform. I loved making little jokes to the crowd about how happy I was with my girl. I swear, I was falling for her more and more each day. At night I would lay my hand on her stomach and silently pray that our baby was growing in there. I knew it was crazy to want a baby with someone I'd just met. But Lexi owned my heart and she was going to be an amazing mother. She was so good at taking care of all of us. She made the bus feel like home somehow.

Things between Lexi and Luke were good. He had stayed true to his word and stopped giving her such a hard time about being with me. And Lex had kept her mouth shut when she saw one of Luke's ex's from high school sneak out of the bus early one morning. Well, she mostly kept it shut. When we stopped for groceries that day she bought Luke some new sheets and told him to burn his old ones. Plus we hadn't seen Lacey again. Luke hadn't even mentioned her name.

Smith was doing really well too. He had picked his groupie habit back up, but thankfully, none of his other vices. We had settled into a routine. After shows Lex and I would head back to the bus to shower and get ready for bed. Either Smith or Jacks would come to our room to get Dagger and take him for a walk before letting him climb into their bunk. They alternated nights. But neither one of them stayed out as late as they used to.

The reporters were getting worse; we had to hire more security. It was like the calmer and more settled we had become, the more eager they were to catch us doing something stupid. We were writing again, all of us together. Jacks would get out his guitar and come up with new riffs; then Smith would join. It was usually Luke and I coming up with lyrics. Lexi would lay her head on my lap and listen to us until she fell asleep. She had started napping over the last week or so. I decided to take that as a good sign. We all watched her every move, silently weighing if it could be pregnancy related or not. It wasn't just me who was excited about the possibility of a baby. All the guys were counting down the days until we'd know for sure.

Chapter Twenty-Five

Lexi

Tonight was the night. I was officially two days late. Dash and I decided that I would wait to take the test until after their show was over. All the guys were so excited. It was so damn sweet. I had agreed I'd take it as soon as we got back to the dressing room that way everyone could be there for the results. The only reason I had said yes was because I was 99% sure it was going to be positive. My boobs hurt so bad I wanted to cry every time I took off my bra. My stomach was hard as a rock, and the smell of Dagger's food made me want to puke. I heard Dash talking over the sound system. "So you all know I have this girl..." The crowd cheered. They loved hearing little snippets about Dash's personal life. He rarely ever did any interviews, none of the guys did. "She's the best thing that has ever happened to me." He played the first few chords of an old Van Morrison song, "These Are the Days," before he started singing he looked over at me. "I love you, Lexi." My eyes filled with tears as I mouthed, "I love you too." He was the best thing that had ever happened to me too. Everything about Dash, about this life I was leading, was unexpected. Unexpected but so damn perfect. The crowd of hardcore rockers sang along to the slow sweet love song.

The show ended a couple of songs later and the guys all ran off the stage. Dash picked me up and buried his face in my neck. "I love you so fucking much, Lex."

I smiled, "I love you too." He sat me down. "That was wooing at its finest."

He laughed, "I aim to please." He took my hand and all but dragged me back to the dressing room. All the guys filed in after us and they shut and locked the door. Smith went over to his guitar case were we had hidden the pregnancy test and tossed it to me.

I went into the bathroom and shut the door. I read the instructions and then took the test. I balanced it on the counter while I washed my hands. It took no time at all for two pink lines to appear. For the second time that night my eyes filled with tears. I looked at myself in the mirror, taking some deep breaths. I was going to be a mom. I was having a baby. Holy balls. I closed my eyes, placed my hand on my stomach and smiled. I knew the guys were probably going crazy out there, but I wanted to savor this one small moment in time when it was just me and our baby.

I opened the door, test in hand. "We're going to have a baby." I loved seeing the smiles on their faces. And I was almost positive they all got a little teary eyed too.

Chapter Twenty-Six

Dash

None of the guys had felt like going out tonight. Everyone was excited about the baby. And I guess they didn't feel like groupies and whiskey were the way to celebrate. Instead we were piled in the living area watching *McClintock!* It was Luke's turn to pick the movie. But he and I both knew this was one of Lexi's favorites. I wanted nothing more than to take Lexi to bed and make love to her until the sun came up. But it seemed like all the guys were feeling extra love towards her tonight so I begrudgingly agreed to the group slumber party. At least until everyone fell asleep. Luke and I sat on opposite ends of the couch with Lexi stretched out between us. She was mostly sitting in my lap—I couldn't seem to get close enough to her lately—but her feet were resting on Luke's legs. Since he had started being more supportive of our relationship, it had become easier for me to see their closeness. Don't get me wrong—I still hated it when he kissed her forehead or walked with his arm around her—but seeing her feet resting in his hands no longer made me want to hit him. Well, not hit him hard enough to hurt him.

When McClintock got himself involved in the huge mud pit fight Jacks leaned his head back to look at us. "So what happens now? Do we need to find Lex a doctor?"

I nodded. "I have one that's going to meet us next week in Florida. We have a couple of days there at a hotel so I figured that would be better than them trying to do everything on the bus."

Lexi turned in my arms. "You called a doctor already? What if it would have been negative?"

I bit my lip to keep from smiling. "Then I would've had the doctor tell us what to do different the next month so that I would have for sure knocked you up."

"Will we be able to see the baby at that appointment or is it too soon?" Smith had paused the movie. I knew his favorite line was coming up and he didn't want to miss it.

Lexi pursed her lips. "I think it'll be too early to see the baby. They'll probably just do a blood test and give me some prenatal vitamins."

Luke put his hand on Lexi's shin. "Should we get a doctor to travel with us?"

I brushed his hand off her leg. "I figured if she liked this doc then we could ask them if they would be willing to meet up with us when it was time for our next appointment."

"We should get a nutritionist too. Help us figure out how to eat better on the road. We need to make sure the baby gets what it needs." Jacks scowled at the bag of Oreos sitting on Lexi's stomach.

She put her hand on top of them and sent Jacks an "I dare you" look.

Smith cocked his head to the side, thinking. "Maybe we should get a trainer too. Prenatal yoga is supposed to be really good for both us and the baby."

I nodded. "You're right. Okay, I'll ask around and see who I can find. We'll probably need to add another bus."

Lexi sat up. "Whoa, whoa, whoa. I'm hearing a lot of 'we's' and 'us's' here, guys. I'm pregnant. I'm cooking this kid. I decide what the baby needs."

I put my hand on Lexi's head, turning her towards me. "Uh, don't you mean *we* decide? I put it in there."

She kissed my neck, but otherwise ignored my question.

Jacks chuckled, "You may be Dash's whole world, Lex, but you're the center of our universe. We would be a mess without you. And that baby? It's part of all of us. We all love it. Hell, most of us heard it being conceived…. You know the rules on the bus—majority vote wins. And you're really out numbered."

Lexi scoffed, "Since when has that been the rule on the bus?"

Jacks raised his hand. "All in favor of making a new rule that states majority vote wins, say 'Aye.'"

Smith, Luke and Jacks all said "Aye."

Jacks grabbed the Oreos off Lexi's stomach and laughed, "Motion passed."

***

I woke up still sitting on the couch in front of the TV. Lexi was curled up against my chest. Luke had fallen over and had his head on her thigh. I resisted the urge to push him off the couch. Barely. Jacks, Smith, and Dagger were sleeping in a pile on the floor. Getting Lex out of here and into bed was going to be difficult. I picked her up, Luke slid down to the couch, and I weaved my way through bodies and pillows and empty chip bags. When I got us to our room, I got Lexi dressed for bed. Which meant I took off all her clothes. I'd be damned if the night I told her I loved her for the first time and found that we were having a baby, would be the first night we didn't have sex. I gazed down at her beautiful body. I knew her breasts had been hurting her for a few days now. When we were in bed she kind of rushed me past foreplay, she never did that before. Her normally flat stomach was hard as a rock—even when she was just lying down relaxing. If Lexi thought I hadn't noticed these things, she was crazy. I knew her body. I'd spent countless hours memorizing every inch of her. The smallest difference would always be apparent to me. I looked up at her face to make sure she was still asleep before leaning down and putting my head by her stomach. I whispered, "Hey little…one, I'm your daddy. So, you'll be hearing my voice a lot. I promise to talk you through all of this. You'll also be hearing a lot from your uncles. They seem pretty hell bent on being part of this experience. You see, we all just love you so much, and we want to make sure that you are always safe and happy. I need you to know that from the moment we knew you were a real possibility, you were wanted. Your mommy is the most amazing girl I've ever met. We are so lucky to have her. I know that a lot of this isn't under your control, but if you could try to take it easy on her in there, I'd really appreciate it." I kissed her stomach. "I'll talk to you tomorrow, little one. Sweet dreams."

Lexi's fingers ran through my hair. "You are going to be the best daddy."

I looked up with tears in my eyes to see her already crying. "I love you so much, Kitten. Both of you. I never knew I could feel this much."

She smiled and tugged me up to the pillows next to her. "I know. It's so surreal and so…I don't know, so wonderful."

I climbed on top of her positioning myself between her legs. I entered her in one practiced motion. She closed her eyes and arched her neck moaning quietly. "Look at me, Lexi." I wanted this time to be different. I wanted her to watch me love her, watch the emotion behind what I was doing to her with my body. It was the most intense sex I've ever had. Every thrust threatened to make me come.

Every moan out of her mouth made chills shoot down my back. "I love you. God baby, I love you."

Chapter Twenty-Seven

Lexi

The hotel where we were staying in Florida was breathtaking. We could walk out the door and instantly have our feet in the powder-soft sand; a few more steps and we'd be in the ocean. It was fall, so it was a little too cold for us to get in the water. Dagger on the other hand jumped in any chance he got. We had gotten a big four-bedroom suite that had a kitchen and living area in the middle. As hard as I tried, I couldn't get the guys out of the suite before my doctor's appointment. I attempted to set up an offshore fishing trip; they canceled it. I tried to get Chase to move their radio appearance up a couple of hours; he said, "No, Lexi, majority rules." And then the guys just happened to reschedule it for the next day. It's not that I wanted to hide anything from them or keep them from this process. But a big part of me wanted to be selfish and keep all these appointments between Dash and I. When I told him how I felt, he promised me that our first sonogram would just be the two of us. I was sitting on the couch, eating an apple since all my cookies had suddenly disappeared, when there was a knock at the door.

I stood to answer it but Smith beat me to it. "Hi, you must be Dr. Solomon. I'm Smith. It's nice to meet you."

A very pretty woman walked into the room carrying a medical bag. She must have been in her fifties. She smiled when she saw me. "I'm guessing you're Lexi? I'm Dr. Solomon."

I took her out stretched hand. "I am. Thank you so much for coming."

"My pleasure, sweetheart." She had kind eyes and warm hands. She looked behind her at Smith. "Are you the father?"

He shook his head, "No…no, no, no."

I rolled my eyes and sat back down on the couch, motioning for Dr. Solomon to join me. When we had both sat, Jacks and Luke walked in. "Guys, this is Dr. Solomon." I pointed to each one in turn. "The blond with the baby face is Luke and the dark haired devil is Jacks."

She smiled. "Hello." She turned to me and dropped her voice. "Uh, is one of them the father?"

I laughed, "No." Thankfully Dash picked that moment to walk in. When he came and sat down next to me, resting his hand on my thigh, I smiled. "This is the baby's father, Dash."

He took her hand in his. "Thank you so much for coming. I know these are unusual circumstances, but with the reporters and paparazzi and touring…" he trailed off.

"It's okay Mr. Conner, I understand." Dr. Solomon looked around the room; all the guys were sitting around us. "Uh, is everyone going to be joining us for this appointment?"

I nodded, "Yes, for *this* appointment, everyone will be joining us." Dash leaned in and placed a kiss on my neck. Dr. Solomon asked when my last period was and when we thought we had conceived. Embarrassingly enough Jacks answered that last question.

She took some blood and gave me samples of some prenatal vitamins. "Start with these. If they make you feel sick call my office and we can see about switching you to something else. I'll call you tomorrow with the results of the blood work. You're next check should be in about five weeks, ten weeks is when we can usually get the baby's heartbeat on the sonogram."

"Like I said, we're touring." Dash rubbed his hands up and down my arms, "Would you, or anyone you work with be willing to travel for those appointments?"

"I wouldn't be able to do that. My patient load is too big. But I do have a PA that works for me that would probably be willing to travel. For routine checks, I'm not really needed. And my PA would call me with any questions or concerns. Just call my office and ask for Dylan."

Jacks raised his hand. Lovely. They were treating this poor lady like a teacher. "We had discussed meeting with a nutritionist. Lexi really doesn't eat all that healthy…." Jacks caught me shooting daggers at him. "What? You don't."

Dr. Solomon grinned. "I always advise my patients to just try and eat as healthy as possible. Lots of fruits and veggies, stay away from sugar, caffeine, and salt, and drink a lot of water."

Smith raised his hand, God help me. "Lexi doesn't really exercise, well, except for the cardio that got her into this condition. We talked about doing some yoga. Is there anything else we can try?"

"Prenatal yoga is a wonderful idea." She looked over at me and winked. Good, at least she thought this was funny and not completely twisted.

Dash raised his hand. I turned and gave him a "what the fuck" look. He just shrugged. "What about sex? Is that safe? I won't…uh…hurt the baby, will I?"

I closed my eyes and let my head fall down to my chest.

Dr. Solomon was full out laughing at this point. "No. No, unless you have a twelve inch penis made out of cement, the baby will be fine."

I snorted trying to hold in my giggles. If Dr. Solomon's PA was anything like her, he'd fit in great around here.

***

The next day I had just come in from a walk on the beach with Dagger when my phone started to ring. I saw that it was Dr. Solomon's office and my heart began to pound. "Hello?"

"Lexi? This is Dr. Solomon. I have the results of your blood work here. Is now a good time?"

"Yes, ma'am, it is. I've been waiting for your call. I have to admit, I'm a little nervous."

"I understand. First time mommies usually are. Everything looks great though, sweetheart. You're HCG and progesterone levels are right where they should be."

"Oh my gosh. I'm so glad to hear that, thank you."

"Dylan told me that Dash called and set up your next appointment?"

"Yes, we'll be in Alabama by then. I guess we are renting a portable sonogram machine?"

"I do think that would be best. It'll be easier to keep it on the bus than it would be for Dylan to try and travel with it."

"Okay, well thank you so much. For everything."

"You're welcome dear. Now, you call me if you have anything questions."

"I will, thank you."

"Good-bye, Lexi."

"Bye."

I immediately texted Dash. He and the guys were at the radio interview, but I knew they'd want to know about the blood work.

Me: Dr. Solomon called. Everything looks great!

My phone buzzed back immediately

Dash: I LOVE YOU (BOTH).

I smiled. Dash had said that to me a hundred times now, and it still took my breath away. My phone buzzed again.

Dash: The band wanted me to tell you to rub your belly for them and that they love you both too.

I laughed and placed my hand on my stomach. "Kiddo, your daddy and your uncles wanted me to tell you that they love you." Tears filled my eyes, for the tenth time today. "I do too. I love you. Please stay safe in there. Just stick with me, okay?"

I wasn't all that close with my family. They weren't bad or mean people. They just weren't very loving. I'd tell them about the baby, eventually. But there was one person I was dying to tell. I went through my favorites and hit Amy's name.

"Lex? Oh my gosh! What the hell?! I haven't talked to you in weeks."

I smiled, typical Amy. "I know, Ams. I'm so sorry. Things here have just been crazy. I have so much to tell you…."

"Start with Lacey. Please tell me she and Luke aren't back together. I'll cut a bitch."

"No. They aren't back together. He did bang her though. I screamed at him. He screamed at me. We made up and she hasn't been around since."

"Okay, good. How are things with Dash? I saw a clip online of him professing his love to you last week. I kept waiting for you to call me!"

"Yeah, I've wanted to call you a hundred times. I just wanted to wait until we were 100% sure…."

"About what?"

"I'm pregnant."

"Shut. The Fuck. Up."

"I will not. I'm like five weeks pregnant so it's really early…but, yeah."

"Oh my gosh, Lex! I am so happy for you guys. Is Dash happy? I mean this wasn't on purpose right?"

"We like to call it our funny little miracle. And he is, he's really happy. Everyone is actually. The guys act like we're all pregnant. They tell me when and what to eat and when and how to work out. They make me nap. It's insane. But in the best way possible."

I heard a bell ring in the background. "Lex, I gotta go, my next class is starting. But I love you so much. Please hug Luke for me. As soon as I can find time, I'm coming to meet up with you guys."

"Love you too, Ams. Call you soon."

After we hung up, I cried again. I missed my friend. I wanted to see her face so badly.

Chapter Twenty-Eight

Dash

One more week to go and I'd get to see my baby for the first time.
Get to hear its heart beating. I was counting down the days. Lexi was
doing well. She got queasy around lunch-time every day, but ginger
ale and peanut butter crackers were the cure. Either every morning or
every night, Lex and Smith would do forty-five minutes of prenatal
yoga. They couldn't do it while the bus was barreling down the
highway—they'd learned that the hard way. Luke and Jacks were in
charge of meals and grocery shopping. All of us had given up fast
food. Hell, I rarely even drank anymore. By the time our shows were
over, Lex was exhausted and just wanted to come back to the bus
and relax. Smith and Jacks kept all the groupies either backstage or
outside. Lex had told them countless times that it didn't bother her
and they could bring girls back to the bus. They said they weren't
doing it for her; they were doing it for the baby. Every single thing
about life on the road had changed. And I fucking loved it. I couldn't
get enough of Lexi. I couldn't seem to touch her enough or kiss her
enough. I sang to the baby every night, always something chill and
calming. My life was…perfect.

***

I stopped dead in my tracks when I saw Jared waiting outside
our dressing room door. I hadn't seen him since we'd kicked him out
of the band over a year ago. I hadn't even heard his voice. It was like
seeing a ghost. "Kitten, come back here please." When I'd stopped
walking, she had kept going. She wasn't even paying attention to her
surroundings; she was too busy taking pictures.

She turned towards me confused. "What?"

I held my hand out, palm facing up. "Can you just come back to
me?"

Luckily she did what I asked. It was hit and miss these days on
whether she took orders or told you to shove it up your ass. She
placed her hand in mine. "Dash, what's going on?"

By then the other guys had caught up to us. Luke slung his arm around Lexi's shoulder. "Why are y'all just standing here in the hallway?"

Jacks and Smith both stopped short just like I had when they spotted Jared. I looked over at Smith. "Did you know he was coming tonight?"

He shook his head. "No, man. I haven't talked to him in weeks. I swear."

Jacks held his hands up. "I haven't had anything to do with him since he left rehab, you know that."

I took a deep breath, this was the last thing we needed right now. Everyone was getting along; Smith was sober—well soberish. I turned to Luke and whispered, "Get Lex out of here. Just take her to another room, I need to make sure Jared isn't here to cause trouble." Luke nodded and grabbed Lexi's hand

When he went to walk away, she resisted. "Dash? What's going on? Is he dangerous? Should we call Chase?"

I put my hand on her cheek. "It's fine, Kitten. Jared is just…unstable. Seeing Luke would upset him." I could tell by the look on her face she didn't really buy it. But thankfully she let Luke lead her and Dagger away.

The rest of us walked over to our old band mate. Smith stuck his hand out to Jared. "Hey, man, long time no see. What are you doing here?"

Jared looked like shit. He was too thin, too pale, too twitchy. We could all see it. "I was in the neighborhood, just thought I'd come catch a show. Check out your new drummer. Who's the chick?"

My fists automatically clenched at my sides. Jacks chuckled, "Oh that's Dash's latest fling. She used to belong to Luke." His words made my blood boil. But I understood what he was doing. If Jared thought Lexi was important to any of us, he'd try to use her against us. "So, you're sticking around for the show then?"

Jared turned to me, scowling. "If that's alright with the boss here."

"Yeah, man. We'd love for you to stay." I wanted nothing more than to kick his junkie ass out of here. But we'd all learned long ago that in order to keep the peace, we just needed to humor Jared. He'd eventually get bored and leave on his own. There were no drug dealers hanging out in the dressing room, no more doing lines off groupies' asses before we hit the stage. Times had changed and these new times would bore him to death.

I took my phone out and sent a quick text to Luke.

Me: Keep Lex away from the dressing room, I'll send Chase to hang out with her so you can get ready.

My phone buzzed back before I had a chance to put it away.

Luke: I can go on in what I'm wearing. I'll stay with Lex.

I opened a new message, this one to Chase.

Me: As soon as we go on, stay with Lexi. Jared is here.

Chapter Twenty-Nine

Lexi

Luke wouldn't let me out of his sight, per Dash's instructions and his own protectiveness. He even came with me to pee. When it was time for them to go on, Chase was supposed to come babysit me but he wasn't anywhere to be found. Dash gave me strict orders to stay on the side stage right where he could see me. I didn't know what the big deal was. I had Dagger with me and everyone who was milling around backstage knew I was with Dash. The crowd was crazy tonight, full of so much for love for the guys. A lot of people were holding up posters and signs. I instinctively reached for my camera before I realized I didn't have it. I must have left it in the dressing room. Dash had been looking over at me every couple of minutes, making sure I was following his orders. But right this second he was over on the other side of the stage jamming with Smith. I could grab my camera and be back before he even noticed. And even if he caught me, I'd just stick my tongue down his throat to keep him from yelling at me. "Come on, Dags. Come with momma."

I looked everywhere for my camera before I remembered I'd never even been in the guys' dressing room tonight. Damn pregnancy brain.

"Lexi? Right?"

Aw, hell. I knew without even looking that it was Jared in the doorway. It didn't know why Dash didn't want me around him, but I knew I was going to get yelled at tonight, tongue or no tongue. "The one and only. And you must be…Jared?"

"My reputation precedes me." He pushed off from the doorframe he was leaning against, walking towards me wearing a really gross smile.

"Nah. The guys never talk about you." His smile turned into something worse. Something way more dangerous. Nice, Lex. Poke the crackhead bear.

"Well they talk about you. You're Dash's new toy…but you used to belong to Luke?"

"Something like that." I felt no need to correct him. He didn't need to know our truth.

"Dash always did like to share. And watch for that matter."
Lovely, my baby daddy was an even bigger whore than I had
thought. Dagger's body got tenser the closer Jared got to us. I
gripped his leash tighter. "But something tells me, he wouldn't like
sharing you." He was standing right in front of me now. Dagger let
out a low growl. I reached down and patted his head. The last thing
we needed was for my giant pit bull to kill the ex-drummer back
stage. That'd be bad press, for both The Devil's Share and Dagger.
"He has been plastering his love for you all over the place."

Jared put his hand on my shoulder, squeezing so hard I had to
bite my lip to keep from crying out. "What is it that you want from
me?" Dagger lunged and snapped at him. It was a warning, if he had
really wanted to break my hold on him, he could have. I scratched
him behind his ears to settle him back down.

Jared's gross sneering smile returned. "I want to feel like part of
the band again. I want to share too." His grip went from my shoulder
to my neck. Dagger growled and snapped. Jared squeezed my neck,
cutting off my airway. I recognized the look in his eye; it was like
déjà vu. He was cracked out of his mind. He pushed me up against
the nearest wall, pressing his knee between my legs. It was difficult
to swallow the bile rising in my throat. This was it, the crossroads. I
could let Dagger's leash go and he could attack Jared. Or I could just
close my eyes and wait until Dash noticed I was gone. I knew what I
should do, what Dash would want me to do. But I was having a hard
time releasing the leash.

"What the fuck is going on?! Jared, get your hands off of her.
Security!" Chase came charging into the room. Jared squeezed my
neck even harder. I saw spots before he backed off with his hands in
the air. "Lexi, oh my God, are you okay?" Two large security guards
came in and grabbed Jared. "Get him off the premises. Make sure he
leaves."

I rubbed my neck. It was sore. I was sure I'd have bruises. My
shoulder too. Damn, Dash was going to be livid. "Yeah, Chase I'm
fine." I got down on my knees, eye level with Dagger. "You are a
good boy. You are such a good boy." I scratched his chest and kissed
his face. I stood up and turned to Chase. "Let's get back out there.
Dash is liable to stop the show. I've been gone too long."

Chase took a deep breath. "Lex, we should press charges. He left bruises. No telling what would have happened if I hadn't come in."

I shook my head, placing my hand over my neck. "I'm fine, really. He's all messed up. Please, Chase, I don't need drama right now. The police and reporters go hand and hand. Just leave it."

He nodded. "Fine. But shit is going to hit the fan when Dash sees your neck, Lex. Be prepared."

When we got back to the stage Dash looked over at me and gave me a not so nice look. I smiled as big as I could and blew him a kiss. When the show ended I mentally braced myself for what was about to happen. I wished I had telepathy so I could warn the rest of the band. I plastered a smile on my face. Dash walked right up to me, grabbed my hand and took off in the direction of the dressing room. I glanced behind me, all the guys were following, and they looked equally as pissed. Damn, so much for any allies. The door shut and locked behind Chase. "What the hell, Lexi? What part of 'don't fucking move' did you not understand? You could have been hurt. Jared could have seen you. Dammit, Lexi." I cut my eyes to Chase, wondering if he was going to tell him or if I should. But my bruises beat us both to it. "What the fuck happened to your neck? Are those bruises?!" He tilted my head back, studying my neck, rubbing his fingers lightly over my marred skin.

Luke came over and joined Dash. When he saw my skin, all the color drained from his face. I knew he was having flashbacks. My heart hurt for him, for both of them. "I came in here to grab my camera and Jared must have followed me. He spouted a bunch of stupid crap, grabbed my neck, and then Chase came in. That's all that happened. And I'm fine."

"Like hell you're fine! Look at you!" Dash closed his eyes and took a few deep breaths. I knew he was trying to calm himself down. I knew he hadn't meant to yell at me. I knew he was just scared. He turned to Chase. "Where is he?! I'm gonna kill him."

Chase put his hands out, placating Dash. "He's gone man. They escorted him off the premises."

Luke put his hand on my shoulder and I winced. He narrowed his eyes. "What? Why does your shoulder hurt? Take your shirt off."

I scoffed, "No, perv." I was trying to break the tension with humor. No one was having it.

Dash grabbed the hem of my shirt. "Take your shirt off, Lexi."

I swatted his hands away, "You don't even let me walk around the bus in a towel and you want me to take my shirt off? No. It can wait until we get back to the bus." I mentally added, and I can take off all my clothes and distract you with a blow job.

Dash shook his head. "I saw you get dressed tonight, Kitten. I know you have a tank top on under that shirt. Now, strip."

At least his tone had softened. I lifted my shirt off with my good arm. I honestly didn't know if I'd be able to raise my other arm above my head—my shoulder really did hurt. Jared was surprisingly strong for an emaciated junkie. Smith and Jacks had come closer. When Smith saw my shoulder he collapsed in a nearby chair. Jacks shook his head and ran his hands down his face. It must have looked as bad as it felt.

Dash leaned in and placed a soft kiss on my shoulder. "Lexi, baby, I'm so sorry. I should have thrown his ass out the moment I saw him. This is my fault."

Smith stood. "No. It's my fault. He's my cousin. I should have tossed him out."

Chase shook his head. "I should have checked my phone sooner. She should have never been alone."

I laughed. "Y'all are all crazy. Jared is gone and I'm okay. Now we know just how dangerous he is. Right? Lesson learned. Please don't go blaming this on yourselves. Hell, I'm the one who didn't listen. It's more my fault than anyone else's." I looked over at Luke. "Lukey, I'm fine. I promise. Please don't let old demons get in your head."

Chase cleared his throat. "Speaking of your fault…why were you holding Dagger back? I could hear him snarling from across the room. Why didn't you let him off his leash?"

Dash looked at me, eyebrows raised in question. "You held him back?"

"If I would have let him go, he would have killed Jared. He would have gone for his throat and not let ago until the job was done. I couldn't let Dagger become a murderer. What would the press say? They would have made me put him down."

Luke laughed humorlessly, "So you were willing to let Jared do God knows what to you, just so Dagger didn't get a bad rep?"

"Bad rep?! We would have had to put him down, Luke."

120

Luke threw his hands in the air. "Dammit, Lex. You're fucking pregnant! Use your head."

I opened my mouth to yell back but Dash held his hand up to stop me. "Luke is right, Lexi. That wasn't a smart move. Let Dagger protect you. Let him do his job. I promise I won't ever let anyone hurt him, okay? We'll hide him away on some ranch somewhere. But if it ever comes down to it, let him protect you."

Chapter Thirty

Dash

Lexi and I were safely back on the bus and my heart rate had finally returned to normal. The rest of the band was here with us. It seemed like no one wanted to let her out of their sight. When it came down to the important stuff, we were a family. And they all loved Lexi, and they all loved the baby. The thought that they had both been in danger upset all of us. Jacks came from the kitchen carrying a bag of Oreos. "Here you go, Lex. I had some hidden in the back of the fridge."

She smiled. "Thanks, buddy." She tore into the bag like a crazy person. Well, like a pregnant chick that had been denied cookies for the last four weeks.

Smith was sitting in the recliner nursing a beer. "You guys want to watch a movie?"

"No." I stood and pulled Lexi to her feet. "I'm taking Lex to bed. She's had a rough night and we'll need to get her shoulder looked at tomorrow morning." We had all tried to convince her to go tonight, but she wouldn't have it. She was so damn stubborn. She told all the guys good night, making sure to pass out hugs and kisses. Usually, it set my teeth on edge. But, tonight, I knew they needed it as much as she did.

As soon as the door shut behind me, Lexi started stripping off all her clothes. "What are you doing?"

She looked over she bruised shoulder and winked at me before climbing into the bed. "Trying to distract you with sex."

I got naked and got in next to her, pulling her body against mine. "Baby, you scared the shit out of me tonight. I wouldn't make it if anything happened to you."

She placed her hand over my heart. "I know. I made some bad choices tonight. From now on, I'll be more careful. Promise." She placed her mouth against mine and nibbled on my lower lip.

Sex had been the last thing on my mind when I had pulled her down the hall to bed. I wanted to hold her close and listen to her breathing even out while she fell asleep. But far be it from me to deny sex to my beautiful girlfriend.

Chapter Thirty-One

Lexi

Luckily Dash had calmed down after a couple rounds of incredibly slow and sweet sex. It was probably the tamest sex we'd ever had. We were lying naked in bed, tangled up together. I loved him so damn much. I hated that I made everyone worry. His hand was lying protectively over my stomach. I couldn't sleep. The realization of what could have happened tonight was keeping my mind from resting. Maybe Jacks had forgotten to re-hide the Oreos… I carefully slid out from under Dash and pulled on one of his t-shirts. It hung down to my thighs, plenty of cover up. Even if it wasn't, this would be payback for making me take off my shirt earlier. I shut the door behind me as quietly as I could and tiptoed down the hallway. I didn't know if the rest of the band was still up or if they were asleep in their bunks. There was a lamp on in the living area, the soft glow making the bus seem so homey. Yes! The bag of Oreos was still sitting on the table where I had left it. I grabbed one and shoved the whole thing in my mouth. Movement outside caught my eye. Smith was standing out there staring up at the stars. I wasn't allowed to walk Dags by myself in the middle of the night, but there's no way I could get in trouble if I went outside while Smith walked him. Plus, I wanted to make sure Smith wasn't beating himself up about the whole Jared incident. I didn't want this breaking him and sending him in search of an escape. I shoved another cookie in my mouth before I opened the door and carefully descended the metal stars. If I so much as stubbed my toe Dash was never going to let me leave the bus again. I called out to Smith, trying to talk around my mouthful. "Hey, bud, whatcha doin' out here?"

Smith glanced at me over his shoulder without turning around. "Go back inside, Lexi."

"Eeeewww…are you getting a blow job out here? And you're letting Dagger watch? What's wrong with you?" I turned to head back to the bus—that was not something I wanted to see. Again.

I heard the unmistakable sound of a gun being cocked. Goose bumps broke out over my whole body. "Don't fucking move. I'll shoot him, right here, right now." I took a deep breath and slowly turned around. Jared was pointing a gun at Smith's chest. It was only then that I noticed that the hair on Dagger's back was raised and Smith was standing with his hands up.

Smith spoke louder. "Go inside, Lexi. Don't worry about me."

Jared chuckled. "When the hell did you become so selfless? What is it with this chick? I need for you to hear me, cousin, and then I'll say who stays and who goes." Jared waved the gun around a little. "Where was I? Oh yes. You stupid mother fucker, you are such a sheep. You let Dash boss you around. You let him make you turn your back on family. What would your daddy say, Smith? He'd beat the shit out of you if he knew what a pussy you've become. I should just put you out of your misery."

Smith nodded. "You're right man. I'm a pussy. I deserve your anger, but Lexi doesn't. Let her go back in and then you and I will fix this. We're family. We should stick together."

Dagger snapped and lunged. Smith held him back. I was rooted in place, not sure what I should do. I could mouth off to Jared, deflect his attention. That wasn't smart. I could make a run for the bus. That could get Smith shot and killed.

Jared looked past Smith to where I was standing. "Get over here and get your damn dog before I shoot him." He pointed the gun at Dagger briefly before turning it back to Smith.

Was he serious? He couldn't be serious. Jared was so far gone; all brain function had stopped. I knew what I had to do even though I didn't want to do it. I walked over to them, mumbling under my breath, "Dumb ass junkie."

"What'd you say, girl?" I hadn't noticed until that moment that Jared had a very backwoods accent.

I put my hand on Dagger's leash. I looked Jared in the eye as I unclicked it. "I said Dumb. Ass. Junkie." Chaos erupted. Dagger lunged for Jared. I heard the sickening sound of flesh tearing. The gun went off. Smith and I both hit the ground. And my world went black.

Chapter Thirty-Two

Dash

I woke up and noticed Lexi was gone about two seconds before I heard the gun go off. I flew out of bed, pulling on jeans as I ran down the hallway. I collided with Luke as he stumbled out of bed. We raced towards the door with Jacks right behind us. When we got outside, Dagger was standing over Jared, his mouth covered in blood. Smith was lying on top of Lexi. They were both still and silent. The only sound I could hear was Jared moaning from under Dagger. Luke and I both went to Lex and Smith while Jacks grabbed Dagger and called 911. Somewhere in the back of my mind, I could hear him relay what was going on and that we needed multiple ambulances. I pulled Lexi's body into my lap. "Baby? Lexi? Baby, can you hear me?" I checked her whole body, looking for signs that she'd been shot. Looking for the reason she was unconscious. It took me several seconds to register the warm wet feeling of blood seeping through my jeans. Her head. The blood was coming from her head. "Oh God, Lexi. Lexi?! He shot her."

Luke had been checking over Smith. "Wait! No, wait. Smith has been shot. It looks like it went in his shoulder and there is no exit wound." He ripped Smith's shirt off to check him. "There was just one gun shot. Right? Right?!" I knew he wanted conformation, but I couldn't find the words. He laid Smith down and scrambled over to Lexi. He checked for a pulse, and pressed his head to her chest. "She's breathing. Her heart is beating. I don't think she was shot. I think she just hit her head when she fell."

In the distance I heard the wail of the ambulance sirens. "Jacks, put Dagger in the bus." Dagger was lying at Lexi's side. He looked like a killer with blood all over his face and neck. I didn't know what he would do right now if another set of men came and took Lexi away.

Jacks grabbed him by the collar. "Come on, Dags. Come on, buddy." Dagger reluctantly got up and went into the bus.

Chase came running up to us. "What the hell happened? Oh my God. It was a gunshot we heard, wasn't it?"

I nodded, still holding onto Lexi with all my might. Forget Dagger, I might freak out when they took her away from me. "Chase, I need you to stay here with Dagger. He's inside. Clean him up. He's covered in Jared's blood. This place is going to be swarming with reporters soon."

Chase was kneeling down, looking at the destruction around him. "Yeah, man. Whatever you need."

The sound of the ambulances got louder and louder until it was almost unbearable. Three different sets of paramedics came running, barking orders and questions. Luke was the one in control. He was the one who stepped up and answered them, directed them. "This one shot this one. Then our guard dog attacked him. The girl seems to have been knocked unconscious at some point. She's about ten weeks pregnant. Everyone has a pulse. Everyone's breathing. But they've all lost some blood."

Luke was so calm, so controlled. Jacks was sitting with his head in his heads. I was crying silently over Lexi's still body, my hands resting on our baby. Please God, let them be okay.

***

I didn't know if the hospital was cold, or if my shaking was from straight fear. Luke, Jacks, and I had been sitting in the sterile waiting room for what felt like days. But looking at my watch I knew it had only been a couple of hours. The cops had come to talk to us. Luke once again had been the only one with enough control to answer any questions. I had never been more grateful for the guy than I was tonight. Jared was going to make it, which pissed me off. I wanted to kill him. He needed an unfathomable amount of stitches. We would all have to testify. Lexi would have to testify. Smith was in surgery. They had to remove the slug. It was a flesh wound, but it was still going to take some time and healing before he could play his bass. We had canceled the next three weeks of our tour. No one had come out to say anything about Lexi. I had the absolute worst thoughts going through my mind. I was terrified she would never wake up. Lexi was…everything. My whole world's happiness was literally wrapped up in her. I hadn't been looking for love. I hadn't been looking for a fairy tale. But I'd found it just the same. I needed her to be okay. I wouldn't survive without her.

"Mr. Conner?"

There was a woman standing in the door wearing light green scrubs. My heart stopped. "Yes?"

"Your girlfriend? She's awake and she's asking for you." The word girlfriend being used to describe Lexi felt wrong. She was so much more than that to me. The lady waited for me to rise on my shaky legs. "If you'll just follow me."

I felt light headed, like I might pass out. The relief that Lexi was awake and talking was over whelming. "Is she okay? The baby? Are you the doctor?"

She glanced over her shoulder. "I'm her nurse. She's okay, the doctor will go over everything with you." She stopped next to a closed door. "This is her. The doctor will be in soon." She left before I could ask her about the baby again.

I closed my eyes and took a few deep breaths. I couldn't go in there looking panicked and scared. I needed to be strong for her. I needed to take a page out of Luke's book. That man was fucking stoic. I pushed the door open slowly. "Lex?" The lighting in the room was dim; it was still too early in the morning for the sun to be up. Lexi was lying in the middle of the bed, her hair spread out all around her. Her eyes were closed; she looked like Sleeping Beauty. "Lexi?" I took her hand in mine, bringing it up to place a kiss in her palm. The bruises on her neck were still visible. I swallowed hard, trying to keep my rage in check. Her eyes fluttered, then opened.

"Hey, you." She smiled. She'd been attacked and then almost shot on my watch. And she was smiling up at me. I didn't deserve her.

"How are you feeling, Kitten?" I kissed her hand again.

"I'm fine. Slight headache. How's Smith?"

"He's okay. He was shot in the shoulder. He had surgery to have the bullet removed."

"And Jared?"

"He's alive." I didn't want to talk about him. I didn't ever want his name to come across her lips. "Was the doctor here? Did you see him?"

She shook her head and placed her hand on her stomach. "No, the nurse said he'd be in soon. That's why I sent her to get you. Dash...I'm so sorry." Her voice broke and so did my heart. "I should have stayed inside. I should have listened. Our baby…I should have listened to you. I'm so sorry."

"Shhhh. Kitten, it's not your fault. Shhh…" I placed my forehead against hers. "Nothing about this is your fault." I kissed her lips gently. "I love you, baby. I was so worried. There was so much blood. I…I love you, Lexi. I love you more than life itself, baby." I was crying now. Tears were flowing down my cheeks unchecked. No part of me cared. I needed her to see how much she meant to me, I needed her to understand.

We stayed that way, heads together and crying until we heard the door open. A man in a long white lab coat and navy scrubs walked in. "Hello, I'm Dr. Hays. I'm the attending here tonight."

I straightened but didn't let go of Lexi's hand. It seemed that neither one of us could find the words to ask the question we were both thinking. The doctor pulled up a stool and sat down on the other side of Lexi.

"So Lexi here has a slight concussion, no skull fractures or anything like that. She cut her head on something when she fell, but she only needed a few stitches. They'll dissolve on their own." He glanced down to the chart in his hand. "We did a sonogram when she came in, the baby looks fine."

Lexi bowed her head and started to cry again, relief making her body sag in bed. I sat down next to her, kissing her head. "Is there anything that we need to be worried about? Any long term issues from the fall?"

"No, there shouldn't be. There was no trauma or bruising to her abdomen. She didn't lose a lot of blood. Blood pressure is perfect. The baby is measuring right on track. Everything looks great."

I let out the breath I'd been holding. "Thank you so much. Can I take her home?"

"I'd like to keep her for a few more hours, just for observation. Would you two like to see your baby?"

Lexi squeezed my hand. "Can we? Our first sonogram isn't for another few days…."

The doctor smiled at her, patting her leg. "Of course you can. I'll send someone in here in a few minutes. But after that, I want you to try and get some sleep."

She nodded, smiling, "I will. Thank you." The doctor walked out, writing in Lexi's chart. They were both okay. I was the luckiest son of a bitch on the planet. Lex jiggled my hand getting my attention. "Hey why don't you go get the guys? That way they can see the baby too."

I raised my eyebrows in shock. "Really? I thought you wanted it to just be you and me the first time?"

"I did. But, after all this, I think they should be here too."

I lifted her chin, kissing her mouth softly.

***

I was sitting on the hospital bed next to Lexi. Luke was down at the foot of the bed and Jacks was standing next to him with his cell phone out to record the sonogram for Smith. I leaned down kissing her head for the hundredth time in the past hour while the nurse squirted some green gel on her stomach. It was funny that tonight was the first time I noticed that her belly was no longer flat.

The nurse put the wand on Lexi, pushing slightly. Our baby filled the screen and seconds later its heartbeat filled the room. I'd like to say that I shed a single manly tear and then kissed my girl. Nope. I bawled like a baby—like heaving sobs. Until you see your child, hear their heartbeat for the first time, you don't know what love is.

Epilogue

Lexi

The band had decided to stay in Alabama for another few weeks. Although Smith and I were cleared to travel, Dash wanted to give us both more time to heal. I was okay with that. The house we rented was fully furnished and large enough for all of us to share. It felt so good to be in an actual home. I'd only known hotels and the bus the past couple of months. It even had a big backyard so Dagger could run around. That dog was our hero and he was treated as such 24/7. He got so many kisses and treats. I had let him do his job, let him protect us. Smith and I had a very long heart to heart when he was released from the hospital. I needed him to know in no uncertain terms that nothing about what happened that night was his fault. He was nothing like Jared; he was nothing like his family. He was willing to die for me that night, and I would never forget that. We were all scared that he'd blame himself and turn back to old habits. But the talk had gone well and he seemed okay. Of course, there weren't any groupies to run to or speed within arm's reach. Another good thing about being in this house.

At first Jacks had been super sweet and let me eat Oreos and cheeseburgers. But that had only lasted a few days, now he was back to handing out dried fruit and carrot sticks.

Luke was fine…always fine. He told me at least three times a day, "I'm fine, Lex." I didn't really believe him, but he'd talk to me when he was ready. You couldn't push Luke to share. I don't think he really knew what to do with his emotions about that night. Luke was the strong one. Dash had described him as stoic and I agreed. Luke has always been able to just shut down and do what needed to be done and leave his heart out of it. But it seemed like this time, it was hard for him to pick his heart back up. He was guarded, waiting for the other shoe to drop.

I was so in love with my baby, and with Dash. I was so happy, so overjoyed at the life I led. It was hard to put into words. When I thought of how different things could have turned out, so many times—if we'd taken a different path, not overslept, not smelled

Jäger—everything that had gone wrong to make everything in my life so right. If I had it to do over again, I wouldn't change one thing.

The band was having lunch with their label. The big bosses had flown in this morning. Dash had put the tour on hold without letting anyone know, and there were apparently some things that needed to be ironed out. The silence in the house was nice. I had just closed my eyes to revel in it when there was a knock at the door. That must be Dylan. The PA Dash hired for my appointments was supposed to arrive today. I opened the door and bit my lip to keep from giggling. Dylan was one of the most beautiful girls I'd ever seen. She had long black hair, full and shiny. Her eyes were light blue and the contrast was striking. Couple that with her tiny waist and hella curves, life around here was about to get fun. "Hi! It's so nice to finally put a face to the name. I'm Lexi, please come in." I smiled holding the door open wide. She had a rolling suitcase and a duffle bag. The mini sonogram machine had arrived yesterday. There was a study off the living room and that's where Dash had put it. "How was your flight? Can I get you something to drink?"

Dylan chuckled, "My flight was okay…crowded. And I'd love a bottle of water if you have one."

"Are you kidding? Bottled water is all these guys will let me drink." Dylan followed me into the kitchen. I handed her the water and then sat down at the large island. "Thank you so much for agreeing to travel for my appointments."

"Oh my gosh, no, thank you. I feel like I live at the office. Getting out to see some of the country is a treat." She placed the cap on her water. "How are you feeling? Any morning sickness? Fatigue?"

I shrugged. "I feel pretty good most days. Maybe a little tired, a little moody. How about you? Tired from the flight? You could take a nap if you want. Or we could watch a movie or go to lunch?"

Dylan laughed again. She had an easy way about her. "I'm okay…."

"I'm sorry. I know I sound like a spaz, but I'm always surrounded by men. It's been so long since I've hung out with another chick." I slapped my hand over my mouth. "See? I called you a chick. Please pity me."

***

When the band got home Dylan and I were half way through watching *Steel Magnolias*. There was a bowl of popcorn balanced between us and we were under a bunch of blankets. It felt so nice to watch a sappy movie with another girl. I hadn't realized how much I missed it. "We're in here, babe!"

Dash walked in the room and out of the corner of my eye I saw Dylan's mouth drop open. I smiled to myself. *Yup, he's gorgeous.* "Hey, Kitten, who's your friend?" He leaned in and kissed me, winking.

"Dash, this is Dylan, our PA. Dylan this is Dash, our baby daddy."

Dash reached over and shook Dylan's outstretched hand. He was smirking. I knew why. "So you're Dylan. This is going to be fun…."

Dylan's smile fell and she took her hand out of Dash's grip. I snorted. "I'm sorry, he didn't mean that in the pervy way it came out. What he meant was that you are so damn pretty and well, there are three very single and constantly horny men that will be falling all over themselves as soon as they see you."

Dylan looked from me to Dash and back again. "Um…I don't really know what to say to that. I'm here in a professional capacity, not to hook up with some sex crazed rock gods."

I started to giggle. "Oh honey, aren't we all?"

Dash poked me in the ribs before pulling me to my feet. "Come on, preggo. We brought some food home." He tucked me against his side, "Dylan, are you hungry? We have plenty and I'm sure the guys would love to meet you."

She looked uncertain. Great, we'd scared my new friend. "Dylan, I understand that you are here for work. And I promise as soon as we eat, we can get to my appointment. I'm sorry if we made you feel uncomfortable." I had basically forced her to hang out with me, and now Dash sounded like she was going to be part of some twisted fantasy island hunger games.

The island in the kitchen was loaded down with barbecue. It smelled so freaking delicious. When we walked in I held back and let Dylan walk in front of me. I wanted to see the guys' reaction when they saw her; Jacks dropped his fork mid-bite, Luke spilled tea down the front of his shirt, and Smith tripped over a barstool. Priceless. "Guys, this is Dylan, she's going to be helping with my

OB appointments. Dylan, this is the rest of the band. Luke is the one cleaning his shirt, Jacks is the one with sauce on his face, and Smith is the one who probably has a bruise on his shin." I peeked over at Dylan. She was smiling, despite herself I'm sure.

After everyone had eaten, and all the guys had flirted mercilessly with Dylan, we headed into the study for my appointment. Dylan turned on the machine and started turning knobs and pushing buttons. I lay down, pulled up my shirt and pushed down my pants. My belly was just barely rounded. Dylan froze with the gel above my belly. "Is everyone staying?"

I sighed, "Yes. It's just easier this way." If I kicked everyone out then I'd have to see their sad puppy dog eyes all day.

"Okay. Well, let's see that baby." She placed the warm gel on my stomach and then pressed down with the wand.

The sounds of the baby's heartbeat immediately filled the air. Dash squeezed my hand. Hearing that strong steady beat brought such a sense of relief. I was always slightly terrified that we wouldn't hear it. First time mom nerves, I guess.

"Everything looks great here, Lexi. Heartbeat is good. The baby is moving around all over the place." She pressed some buttons and printed out a couple of pictures. "Your blood pressure is good. Your weight is good. You two are the picture of health." She wiped the gel off my stomach and I sat up. "Now, do you have any questions? Any concerns?"

I opened my mouth to speak, but Smith beat me to it. "I feel like her energy level is way down. I can't get her out of bed most mornings to do our yoga."

Dylan's eyebrows rose past her hairline. She glanced at me. I rolled my eyes. Before she could answer Smith, Jacks started in, "And she could definitely eat better if you ask me."

I narrowed my eyes at him. "Good thing no one asked you then."

Luke leaned forward in his chair. "I think she's having too much sex."

Oh good Lord. "Luke, that really isn't—"

"She cramped up really bad the other night. Is that normal? I googled it but—"

Dash cut Luke off mid-sentence. "What? When did you get cramps? Why didn't you tell me? Why does Luke know?"

I put my hand on Dash's chest. "You fell asleep. I got a cramp. I went to the kitchen to get some water. Luke was on the couch watching a movie. I had to lie down for a few minutes. He asked. It was no big deal. It didn't last long at all."

Dash ran his hands down his face. "Lex. You need to tell me these things." He stood up and started to pace. Huge over reaction if you ask me. "I think we should get a full time nurse. Dylan, would you be willing to do that?"

I threw my hands in the air. "You are being ridiculous. It was one cramp! After sex, one time. It hasn't happened again and—"

Dash turned to Dylan, ignoring me. "We'll pay you ungodly amount of money. All your travel expenses, meals, everything."

"Dash! Stop offering people 'ungodly' amounts of money so they'll do what you want!"

"Why? It worked with you." He winked at me.

I opened my mouth to protest, but all the guys started talking at once. It was hard to decipher exactly what was being said. I heard things like dangerous penis, gestational diabetes, and hypnobirthing. I just leaned back and closed my eyes. I didn't have the energy or the desire to deal with this right now. I wanted a cookie and a nap.

Suddenly a shrill whistle pierced the air causing everyone to quiet. I peeked through one eye. Dylan was standing with her hands on her hips. "That's enough! You four are fucking insane. Last time I checked, which was three minutes ago, there is only one baby in there. Which means there is only one daddy. While I'm sure you all love Lexi and that kid, you are being ridiculous. She is healthy, she eats well, and the fact that she does yoga at all is wonderful. She's doing a great job. Now leave her the hell alone."

I reached out and grabbed Dylan's hand. "Please stay and be my full time person."

The End…ish

AUTHOR'S NOTE

Hey guys! Thanks for reading *Play Nice*, book one of The Devil's Share. *Play Fair*, book two is already in the works and I can't wait for y'all to read Smith's story. I would love nothing more than to hear from my readers. Tell me what you love about your favorite characters and what you wish for them. Check out my website at www.lpmaxa.com

Love,
L.P.

ABOUT THE AUTHOR

L.P. lives in Austin, Texas, with her husband, daughter, three rescue dogs, one stray cat, and one fish (that keeps dying and she keeps replacing so her toddler doesn't notice). She loves reading romance novels as much as she loves writing them. L.P. feels like inspiration can come from anywhere: a song lyric, a quote, a weekend with friends. The tiniest things can spark amazing stories.

Did you enjoy this book? Drop us a line and say so! We love to hear from readers, and so do our authors. To connect, visit www.boroughspublishinggroup.com online, send comments directly to info@boroughspublishinggroup.com, or friend us on Facebook and Twitter. And be sure to check back regularly for contests and new releases in your favorite subgenres of romance!

Are you an aspiring writer? Check out www.boroughspublishinggroup.com/submit and see if we can help you make your dreams come true.

Made in United States
Orlando, FL
11 May 2022